Dragonfly vs Monarch

Book One

by

Charley Brindley

charleybrindley@yahoo.com

www.charleybrindley.com

Edited by

Karen Boston

Website https://bit.ly/2rJDq3f

Front cover art by

Niki Vukadinova

Back cover art by

Charley Brindley

This book is dedicated to

Vern Franklin Brindley

Other books by Charley Brindley

1. *Oxana's Pit*
2. *The Last Mission of the Seventh Cavalry*
3. *Raji Book One: Octavia Pompeii*
4. *Raji Book Two: The Academy*
5. *Raji Book Three: Dire Kawa*
6. *Raji Book Four: The House of the West Wind*
7. *Hannibal's Elephant Girl, Book One*
8. *Hannibal's Elephant Girl, Book Two*
9. *Cian*
10. *Ariion XXIII*
11. *The Last Seat on the Hindenburg*
12. *Dragonfly vs Monarch: Book One*
13. *The Sea of Tranquility 2.0 Book One: Exploration*
14. *The Sea of Tranquility 2.0 Book Two: Invasion*
15. *The Sea of Tranquility 2.0 Book Three*
16. *The Sea of Tranquility 2.0 Book Four*
17. *The Rod of God, Book One: Tthe Edge of Disaster*
18. *Sea of Sorrows, Book Two of The Rod of God*
19. *Do Not Resuscitate*
20. *Henry IX*
21. *Qubit's Incubator*

Coming Soon

22. *Dragonfly vs Monarch: Book Three*
23. *The Journey to Valdacia*
24. *Still Waters Run Deep*
25. *Ms Machiavelli*
26. *Ariion XXIX*
27. *The Last Mission of the Seventh Cavalry Book 2*
28. *Hannibal's Elephant Girl, Book Three*

See the end of the book for details about the others

Contents

Chapter One

In the air over Rio

Current day

Autumn Willow watched the ground below as the old B-17 bomber banked smoothly into the Rio de Janeiro landing pattern. She sat in the right seat of the cockpit and scanned the horizon as they leveled out.

"There's Pantanal 413." She pointed half-left toward the Brazilian Boeing 737 airliner, eight miles to the northwest and five thousand feet above them.

Her grandfather nodded and turned his attention back to the Aerovias cargo jet ahead of them in the landing pattern. He reached to the trim control knob while keeping his eyes on the cargo jet, adjusting the trim by two notches.

"Rio tower," Autumn said into the microphone of her headset. "B-17 388. We've turned downwind behind Aerovias 856."

"B-17 388. Rio tower. We are having you in our sight. Pantanal 413 and American Airlines 221 will circulate once on ten thousand over our heads to serve you time."

"Rio Tower. B-17 388. Relay our thanks to 413 and 221. Sorry we can't match their speed."

"Rio Tower. They think they do not mind idling for one time longer, more or less."

Autumn pressed her radio button twice.

"Pantanal 413 to B-17 388. We just sit on here to enjoy the sight of you aeroplane."

"American Airlines 221 to B-17. You're the prettiest thing I've ever seen in the air."

"Thanks, 221 and 413," Autumn said, then glanced up toward American Airlines 221, ten thousand feet above. "Hope to meet up with you guys on the ground."

"413. We be on there pretty quick afterward you do."

"221. Bet on it. Are you the one flying that graceful old war bird?"

Autumn looked at her grandfather and saw him give her a wink. The old man then took his hands from the wheel and gave her a *Your turn* gesture.

She shoved the microphone up away from her lips. "You kiddin' me?" She grabbed the wheel and lifted her feet to the pedals. "Are you kidding me?"

"I never kid anyone, Clicker. I'm just going to enjoy the ride on this landing."

The twenty-two-year-old grad student swallowed and reached for the four throttles with her left hand. "You work the flaps and carburetor heat for me."

"Tell me when, and how much."

Autumn positioned the microphone back to her lips and pressed her microphone button on the wheel. "Roger that, 221."

"B-17, looks like you got quite a crowd down on the tarmac. Show 'em what real flying's all about."

Autumn pressed her microphone button twice, then called the controller at the airport. "Rio tower. B-17," she said. "Wind check."

She'd seen the airport's tetrahedron pointing into the wind and knew she would have to touch down at a slight angle to the runway, but her grandfather's words came back to her.

Never believe anything you hear, and only half of what you see. Flying is as much art and instinct as it is a science.

"B-17," the tower answered. "Crosswind quartering, left by right. Fifteen knots, approx."

"Roger, tower."

Autumn scanned her instruments and added a little power. The deep throb of the four propellers increased as the engines revved up a tick. She then banked the B-17 into a sweeping right turn.

When you're in the air, there is no wind, because your aircraft becomes part of it. Her grandfather's words from her first flying lesson. *But on landing, you have to deal with the wind aggressively. Otherwise, it'll wreak havoc on the most powerful of aircraft.*

Aerovias 856 cargo was well ahead of the B-17 and already turning cross wind.

Rio de Janeiro's Galeao International Airport, on Governor's Island, has one of the most difficult pilot approaches in the world. With notorious crosswinds and the waters of Guanabara Bay off each end of the runway, there's no margin for error.

Autumn pressed her intercom button. "Buckle up, guys. Guess who's taking the Shenandoah into Rio?"

"Oh, shiiiiiit," someone's voice came over the intercom from the back of the plane.

"You got your 'chute on, Andy?" said another voice.

"I do now."

"Matthew, whar y'all put my dang jug of Jim Beam?"

"Cute," she said and clicked off the intercom as she scanned the horizon for other traffic and banked the old bomber into the downwind leg of the landing pattern.

Aerovias 856 was now on his final approach and would soon touch down on runway two-eight.

Autumn saw the cargo jet crabbing to his left. She felt a bead of sweat collect on her right temple and run down her cheek. She checked the airspeed indicator and altimeter, then pulled all four throttles back a fraction. She eased the wheel forward.

"Ten percent flaps."

"Ten percent flaps." Her grandfather adjusted the flaps.

"Carburetor heat half."

He pushed the four carburetor heat knobs forward. "Carburetor heat half."

She wanted desperately to see his expression but knew she'd read nothing there, even if he was terrified. Outside the cockpit, he always joked, treating her like one of the boys, and he never missed a chance to brag about his granddaughter being a graduate student, studying micromechanics at MIT. But inside the cockpit, he was a serious, no-nonsense pilot all the time.

Grandfather Baylor Willow, two years older than the Shenandoah, was born in 1941. By the end of World War II, the old aircraft had flown forty-six missions over Germany, while he still played with his alphabet blocks. He saved her from the scrap heap in 1964, and now she was one of only eleven left in the world. Of the twelve thousand built during the war, all the others had either been destroyed in battle or scrapped later.

The beautiful vintage plane drew a large crowd everywhere she went, and Autumn couldn't be prouder than to be at the controls as they flew into the Rio airport.

"Landing gear down," she said.

Her grandfather flipped the switches to lower the main gear.

She heard the hydraulics squeal to life and, ten seconds later, the solid thump of one of the wheels locking into place. She waited for the second one, but it didn't happen. Another five seconds, and still no thump. She looked at her grandfather.

His only reaction was to lift a shoulder. *You're in command, Clicker.*

She knew that was his silent response. He always called her by her nickname when they were alone. On her eleventh birthday, he'd given her an old telegraph hand key and wired it into her CD player's speakers so she could learn Morse Code. Autumn thought it was the grandest present she'd ever received and was soon clicking out simple messages for him. She spent so much time on the key, he soon began calling her 'Clicker.' The nickname stuck, but it was their private nickname; everyone else called her 'Autumn.'

Grandfather Baylor was the only father she'd ever known. Her first and second sets of parents were nothing more than blank spaces at the beginning of her life.

She received her first flying lesson from him when she was tall enough to reach the plane's pedals. That was his present to her on her ninth birthday, just ten days after her grandparents had adopted her—her second adoption. Now she had almost three thousand hours in the air; twenty-four hundred in her grandfather's Cessna 150, two hundred in a Link trainer, and the rest in multi-engine aircraft, including two hundred hours at the controls of the B-17. However, she'd never landed the four-engine antique aircraft at a busy major airport.

Autumn flipped her intercom button. "Anderson.

Drop into the ball turret, and check the landing gear.”

“Roger, Captain.”

“Ready on the hand-crank, Williams,” she said.

“I’m on it.”

“Right gear down and locked,” Anderson reported from the ball turret. “Left gear froze halfway.”

“Crank it down, Williams.”

“Roger that.”

“Anderson?” she asked.

“Not moving yet.”

“Thirty percent flaps,” she said.

Her grandfather increased the flaps and looked out his left window to see that the flaps responded. “Thirty percent flaps.”

“The wheel moved down about three inches,” Anderson said over the intercom.

“Rio tower to B-17. We thinking you have only one wheel sticking out.”

“Roger, tower. We’re working on it.” She switched to the intercom. “Come on, Williams,” Autumn said. “We got two minutes to touchdown.”

“You might...” Williams paused to take a quick breath as he worked the manual crank, leaving on his microphone, “have to do a one...wheelie.”

“Yeah, right,” Autumn said. “If you make me go around for a second try, I’m gonna be really pissed. They’re already stacking airliners over our head.”

“I like it better...when Grandpa flies. He’s not so–”

“Crabby?” Anderson cut in.

“Mean?” someone else chimed in.

“Bitchy...is what I was...”

“Ten degrees to go,” Anderson said. “You can line up on final, Ms. Captain.”

“Yeah, when I hear a clunk, I’ll line up on final.”

"Clunk."

"Shut up, Matthew," she said.

"Five more degrees," Anderson said.

Autumn turned into her final approach to the runway. "If I hit the throttles, give me full carb heat and no flaps."

"Roger that," her grandfather said, resting his fingertips on the flap control lever.

Autumn heard a satisfying thump from the left landing gear locking into place, and she began to breathe again. She then flexed her knees to get the circulation going in her lower legs.

"Thirty seconds to touchdown," she said into the intercom and knew the guys would keep quiet now and get into their seats as she concentrated on the landing.

Suddenly, she heard a new sound; something above her head clinked three times and rattled, like a small metal shaft breaking apart. Then came the decreasing whine of a motor winding down. She looked out her right window at the two starboard engines; they looked fine. She leaned forward to see past her grandfather and checked the two port-side engines. He did the same thing. All four engines appeared to be in full operation. She scanned her instrument panel and glanced out over the nose at the runway that seemed to grow larger by the second.

I'm coming in too fast.

On her second scan of the instruments, she saw it: the number two fuel pressure gauge needle touched the zero, bounced a little, and fell to the peg. The other three gauges all hovered around eighty psi.

"Port engine, inboard," she said. "Fuel pressure dropped to zero."

Her grandfather jerked around his head to check the engine. "Still running, but not for long."

"I'm feathering port inboard. Airspeed?"

She knew she could land on two engines if she had to, but she wanted three. From here on in, she'd concentrate only on the runway. Touchdown was less than fifteen seconds away.

"Airspeed one-eighty," her grandfather said.

She eased back the throttles. "Eighty percent flaps."

"Eighty percent flaps."

Autumn felt the increased lift right away and wiggled the pedals to feel the rudder. She watched the nose move back and forth in reaction to the rudder, then eased down the left pedal while applying right pressure to the wheel.

Ten seconds to go.

She had the nose into the crosswind, about five degrees to the left of their forward motion. The instant the two main gears touched the concrete, she'd have to correct the attitude of the plane immediately and align the nose with the yellow center stripe of the runway; otherwise, she risked losing control and running off the runway—or worse, flipping the aircraft over.

Three seconds to go. Two seconds.

Autumn heard the screech of rubber against the rough cement as both main wheels touched down together. Using the pedals and wheel in coordination, she lined up the nose on the center stripe.

"Full flaps," she said.

"Full flaps."

She pulled the three throttles all the way back and eased the wheel toward her stomach to settle the tail wheel down to the runway.

"Speed?" she asked as she concentrated on controlling the roll out.

"One hundred and ten."

She couldn't apply the brakes until they slowed to seventy miles per hour. If she hit the brakes now, she risked burning out the brake linings and possibly starting a fire in the main landing gear. She had plenty of runway ahead of her, so she let the fifteen-ton aircraft slow itself.

"Rio tower to B-17. Please receive taxiway 14-R, at ahead on your right hand."

"Roger, tower."

The problem with a B-17 on the ground is, the pilot can't see directly ahead because the tail is on the cement and nose is raised high in the air—a normal situation for any tail-dragger.

Autumn used the pedals to fishtail a little to see forward. "There's 14-R, two hundred yards."

"Speed ninety," her grandfather said.

The plane slowed quickly now. When the speed fell below seventy, she tilted the pedals forward, applying the brakes, decreasing to fifty miles an hour. When she was within forty yards of 14-R, she braked more and took the turn to her right, revving the outboard port engine to help pull her around and off the runway.

Autumn turned to her right window to see the American Airlines Boeing 777 touch down on the far end of the runway.

"Wow," she whispered, looking back at the taxiway. "He sure had confidence in me."

Her grandfather slid open his window for some fresh air and reached to pat her shoulder. "So did I, Clicker. So did I."

She glanced at him and saw the gray Oxford shirt she'd bought for him in Buenos Aires was soaked with sweat.

Chapter Two

On that same day, on 9th Avenue in New York City, Rigger Entime left an office building and tried to remember where he had parked his car.

He was ten paces beyond the little girl before the image of her eyes registered on his foggy perception of that cold December afternoon—the end of his longest day. His doctor had put him through the stress and strain of a raw recruit. He was exhausted, and he wanted it finished; all of it.

When he turned back toward the girl, an enormous baldheaded man with a cane in one hand and the Wall Street Journal tucked under his arm, bumped into him. Rigger stumbled but kept his grip on the gray slips of paper in his hand.

"Drunken fool," mumbled the bald man as he straightened his overcoat and trudged on.

From a distance, the girl's eyes looked both melancholy and almost gleeful. It seemed to Rigger her sadness was a tender veil, a valiant attempt to disguise her urge to play with the Barbie doll tucked in the crook of her arm.

Her fingers toyed with a bare plastic foot as she stared at Rigger. The doll's other foot was stockinged in faded blue and covered by a tiny black slipper, with the strap swinging loose.

A cardboard sign hung around the little girl's neck, lettered in childish crayon, "Wil work 4 food." Some imprinted words were torn in half along the bottom edge of the cardboard, "It's the real thing."

Past, present, and future fused into a frozen tide of emotion. The Earth lumbered on toward the winter solstice, and compassion warmed his aching heart. Rigger stuffed the five slips of paper into his coat pocket and knelt before her on one knee, feeling the icy cement through his tweed.

"What kind of work do you do, sweetheart?" He guessed she was about four years old.

The woman standing next to the girl spoke a daggered, "God bless you" to the back of a departing pedestrian who'd dropped two coins into her outstretched hand. She shifted her weight from one foot to the other and slipped her hands into the pockets of a dark Navy pea-jacket, the type one might buy for two dollars at a military surplus store. The outline of a torn-off chevron marked the shoulder of the jacket's right arm. Her legs were bare below a short skirt. Thin socks and castoff Nikes rounded out her collection of old clothes. She stared up the street, over Rigger's head, where a lady dressed in sable left a jewelry shop and came their way. Slick crimson nails tucked a fur collar tight over a harness of jewels.

A hand slipped from the pea-jacket pocket.

Rigger carefully fastened the strap on Barbie's shoe as he watched the child's face. He knew it would take only a wisp of a breeze to topple her into his arms, where he could hold her close until she was warm and cozy.

"Can you drink hot chocolate with little marshmallows?" He smiled, trying to soften his expression.

He saw her face start to brighten, but then she caught herself and looked up at the woman. Rigger looked up, too. The woman ignored them as her eyes followed the sable. The eyes of the sable focused on some distant point where parallel lines came together. She elevated her nose and quickened her step.

An empty hand returned to the pea-jacket pocket.

The girl's mother didn't look down at the two people at her feet, but instead shifted her gaze to a young man getting out of a taxi and motioning the driver to keep the change.

"How about you, ma'am?" he said up to her. "Could you go for a cup of hot chocolate?"

She looked down at him, and he saw only bitterness. Not the slightest trace of happiness was in the woman's face, hidden or imagined; perhaps there never had been. The shrug of her slim shoulders conveyed much more than 'I don't care.' She said without a word that she hated him and every rich bastard who walked by and insulted her with a few tarnished coins. Yes, she would take his stingy offering of a hot drink, but only because she and the girl hadn't eaten anything all day. That's what he saw in her cold shrug.

* * * * *

"I help Mommy clean 'partments," the little girl said after a sip of the hot chocolate. She gave her sweet brown mustache a lick.

The three of them sat in a window booth at Hannibal's Cafe, three blocks from where he met them. They were on one side of the table while Rigger faced them on the other. He slipped off his coat and let it fall behind his back. The woman and girl kept their coats on and buttoned.

"Oh," he said, warming his hands on the steaming mug. "I bet you're a big help to Mommy."

The girl nodded as she held a sticky marshmallow to Barbie's lips for a second, then popped it into her own mouth. She picked up her cup and slurped another marshmallow. Her mother stared out the window, with her hands wrapped around an untasted mug of hot chocolate.

Rigger looked to see what held her attention and was startled to meet her eyes in the reflection of the glass. She watched him in the mirrored window, not shifting her gaze. He blinked and took up his cup.

"We gonna get a pet l'phant," the little girl said to Rigger.

The woman looked at the girl, narrowing her eyes. The girl narrowed her eyes back at her.

Rigger tried to interpret this fragment of intercepted communications. Was it a secret that the girl wanted a pet and strangers shouldn't be made aware of it? Was 'pet elephant' a code phrase for something forbidden, perhaps an exotic bird, or maybe a father? Whatever it was, Rigger envied their easy relationship.

"Hurry up with your chocolate, Mama," her mother said. "We have to go."

"So," Rigger said, "you do cleaning work."

"Wait, don't tell me." The caustic knife of her words formed with practiced precision and cut without qualm. "You just remembered your maid went on vacation."

"No, I don't have a maid." He kept his voice soft in spite of her combative attitude.

Has life been so difficult for her that every man is a threat? Or perhaps a menace to something close to her? Why can't she see she has nothing to fear from me?

"Then your apartment is suddenly very dirty." It sounded like an accusation.

"As a matter of fact, I keep it fairly clean." This exchange was wearing Rigger down and getting them nowhere.

"What, then?"

"I just wondered how much you charge?"

"All that the traffic will bear." Her cold eye-lock never wavered, never weakened.

"Oh."

"Isn't that what you charge?"

"I don't charge anything, since—"

"I guess you just live off the fat of the land."

Rigger gave up. "I suppose so."

He returned his gaze to the little face framed in yellow curls and smiled as the girl silently admonished Barbie about something she apparently said without asking the girl's permission.

I wonder if her hair is naturally curly. If not, someone spent a lot of time on it. Unusual for street people.

The woman sipped her chocolate, licked her upper lip, then took a big drink. She followed Rigger's gaze to her daughter, who tried to catch a marshmallow with her tongue.

Ten minutes later, outside Hannibal's, Rigger watched the two of them walk away. The girl hung on to the bottom edge of the pea-jacket as the woman shoved her hands into the pockets. Only the Barbie doll, cradled against the girl's shoulder, looked back at him. He waved goodbye to Barbie, sighed, and went the opposite way. As he walked toward the drug store, he took the doctor's prescriptions from his coat pocket.

* * * * *

On the following Tuesday, the day after Christmas, Rigger walked the streets. He really had no reason to return to Hannibal's Café; he just wanted to taste the chocolate again.

He caught his breath when he saw the two of them across the street from Hannibal's, working the busy lunchtime crowd. They wore the same clothes as last week. He hustled through the traffic while they watched a gaggle of stockbrokers in pinstripes waddle by, half of them with cellphones grafted to their ears, hands attached. The rest of them had Bluetooth earbuds. All of them chattered a bit too loudly and waved their hands in the air, very much full of themselves.

"Hi there," he said, coming up on their blind side.

The woman jerked her head around toward him, almost smiled, but then took on an expression that could have said, *I was actually expecting someone else.*

The child had a new sign, "Please help. Mommy lost job." The girl's face was stony as before, but her eyes welcomed him, and she turned Barbie his way. The doll gave him a blue-crayoned smile that wasn't there last week.

He returned Barbie's smile, then spoke to the mother. "How's business?"

An urge to grab her shoulders to keep them from shrugging rose from his pectorals and tingled down to his hands, creating an awkward gesture. But she surprised him, and for an instant he thought he saw an unguarded sign of relief in her eyes.

"Not bad." No shrug.

"You two had lunch?"

"Nope," she said.

"I'm on my way to see what Hannibal has on today's special. Wanna join me?"

She glanced down at the girl. "You hungry, Mama?"

The child nodded vigorously.

"Well, then, let's go."

Rigger stepped around the woman and picked up the girl before either of them could change their minds.

She was light as a new kitten in his arms. Without hesitation, she put her arm around his neck and held on.

They threaded through the traffic, and he opened the door for the woman to precede him into the cafe.

The waitress told them the day's special was liver, and Rigger noticed an expression of yuck on the child's face. They ordered from the menu, and the waitress scurried away to the kitchen.

Rigger spoke to the girl. "What's your name?"

"Rachel. I'm in the Bible, you know. This is Henry." She held the grinning Barbie doll out to him.

"Hello, Henry." He shook the outstretched plastic hand and felt the texture of her coral and rose pinafore—three doll-sizes too large. "I'm glad to meet you, and I must say, that's a very pretty dress you're wearing."

Rachel stared at Henry, listening for a moment while adjusting the garment over an exposed shoulder. "She likes yours, too."

Rigger studied the girl's face. *Rachel—Appearance - 10, Likability - 10, Attitude - 8, Usefulness - 2.*

"Okay, here's the deal," the woman said, without warning.

Rigger and Rachel looked at her. So did Henry.

"We'll clean your stupid apartment, but it'll cost you fifty bucks."

The girl and Henry looked at Rigger, expectant expressions on their faces.

He savored the moment, feeling some sort of perverse victory over the woman. Had he penetrated her icy facade and touched a warm current of femininity?

Street Woman; Appearance - 8, Likability - 1, Attitude - 0, Usefulness - 6.

"Sorry," Rigger said, thinking he might persuade her to lighten her attitude. "My maid came back from vacation.”

“Let's go, Rach.” She grabbed the girl's arm, pushing her to the edge of booth.

“Wait.” He was no match for her. “Kidding. I was only kidding.” He reached for her wrist to keep them from leaving.

She glared at his hand, then wrenched away hers and settled back to her place. “Don't fool with me, Rigger. I don't play jokes.”

“All right, I'm sorry...” He stopped, confused for a moment. “I just wanted to see you smile.”

“I don't do that either.”

He looked down to see Henry slowly turn her smiling face toward him.

“Okay,” he said. “No jokes, no smiles. I got it.”

The woman held her hand out to him, palm up.

“What?” he asked.

“Payment in advance.”

“Yeah, right...” He saw one eyebrow go up. “Okay, okay. Payment in advance. No jokes, no smiles.”

When his checkbook came out, she shook her head.

“American Express?” Rigger had reached a point where she was either going to take a joke or they were going to end this mercenary affair.

“Actually, I can do American Express.”

“Didn't she say no jokes?” he asked Rachel, then looked the question at Henry. They both nodded.

“You have to add ten percent,” the woman said. “We do it at Punky's Pawn Shop, over on Forty-third.”

“Seriously?”

“You don't think a street woman can do business?”

“Oh, I think you're a businesswoman all right. A very good businesswoman.”

He took some currency out of his wallet, riffling the

18

new twenties to separate them. When he passed two twenties and a ten to her, he looked up to see the waitress glancing from the money to him to the woman.

She shrugged and asked, "Meatloaf?"

He made room for her to set the plate before him. She placed the chicken-fried steak in front of the woman, dropping it from a height that made an annoying clatter, but not quite enough to break the plate. Rachel got a hamburger with a side order of M&Ms, gently.

Henry sat down on the table, with her legs splayed out. She watched Rachel pick out three green candies. One went into Henry's lap.

Rigger picked up his fork and stared at it as if he'd forgotten what he was going to do with it.

When did I tell her my name?

Chapter Three

Rigger's apartment on Central Park East, facing Sheep Meadow.

Rigger roused himself from semi-paralysis and reached for his remote control to pause the Mozart. He hit the wrong button, bringing the TV to life.

A newscast blinked on. "...missing from her morning dance class." A video of a hysterical mother pacing in front of an old redbrick building popped onto the screen. "No one, *no one*, especially Rudolf, my dumb-ass ex-husband, is supposed to pick up my daughter. I've told them and told them, he's an imbecile, he'll grab her and take off to Albuquerque or someplace. I bet he did it. I know the sonofa—"

The video of the woman abruptly changed to the contrite, chiseled face of a young news anchor with much-too-blue contact lenses. He squinted to read the teleprompter.

"However, the Tiny Tyke Academy's spokesperson told our reporter that Samantha Ann Cramer wasn't picked up at the school. They had no record of her arriving for her regular Wednesday morning bullet..." the man stopped and blinked at the camera. "Ah...uh..." he stammered, clearing his throat. "I mean ballet, her Wednesday morning ballet class. The mother insisted she had dropped off the four-year-old girl at nine a.m., as always, and watched her until she was inside the building. Meanwhile, police and child welfare authorities began—"

Rigger clicked off the TV when his doorbell chimed. He opened the door to see the familiar pea-jacket, Henry the Barbie doll, and sweet Irish eyes of Rachel.

"Come in, come in." He stepped aside and waved them into his apartment, imitating the enthusiasm he wanted to feel.

When he closed the door, a fluffy ball of fur came bounding around a corner on the opposite side of the large living room. The puppy tripped on the red ribbon trailing from his neck, tumbled down the four carpeted steps, landed on his head, rolled end-over-end, and jumped to his feet. With tiny pink tongue flapping out the side of his mouth, he ran straight for the girl.

"L'phant!" she cried and ran behind the woman. He chased after her. Rachel dodged away. "L'phant, l'phant!" she squealed. "Save me."

On the third time around, the woman grabbed the girl and held her up high. The puppy sat, panting, looking up at the child, still wanting to play.

"What the heck do you think you're doing?" She didn't give Rigger a chance to answer. "If I wanted her to have a dog, I'd buy her a dog. And it wouldn't be a scruffy mutt like this one." She shoved away the puppy with her foot.

Instead of being rebuffed, the dog took it as an invitation. He yipped happily, pouncing on the woman's foot.

Rachel squirmed around to watch him.

"Who said it was for her?" Rigger asked.

"Oh, so it's your dog?"

"Yes. I've been thinking for a long time I needed a watchdog."

She blew out a breath through pursed lips and shoved away the puppy again. "You call that a watchdog?"

Rigger nodded.

"What's his name, then?"

"I call him...um..." He glanced down at the playful tan and white half-spaniel. "Wolf. His name is Wolf."

"Wolf?"

"Yes."

"Well, if you'll take your vicious watchdog named 'Wolf' and lock him in a closet or something, I'll put Rachel down and get to work."

"All right." Rigger knelt down, swallowing his pain and moving as smoothly as a twenty-eight-year-old man should have been able to. He picked up the little dog. "Come on, pup. You can play in the bathroom for a while."

Wolf—Appearance - 10, Likability -10, Attitude - 10, Usefulness - 0.

When he came back from putting the dog in the upstairs bathroom, he found Rachel standing in the middle of the living room, gazing at the artwork.

"Henry likes your pictures." She turned the Barbie doll toward Rigger.

"Thank you, Henry."

Rigger watched the woman remove her coat, drape it over a chair-back, and take a bibbed apron from her handbag. The apron still had a K-Mart price tag attached. She yanked off the tag, stuffed it into her pocket, slipped the neck strap over her head, and tied the apron strings in the back. Her apricot blouse contrasted nicely with the short tan skirt. It wasn't the same outfit she wore before. Neither were her red peep-toe pumps.

"I'll start in the kitchen. That's always the worst."

She didn't wait for a response before walking away toward the formal dining room, which opened onto a large sunny kitchen. Her heels tapped across the hardwood floor that shimmered under a new coat of wax.

Rigger sat on the edge of his chair and looked at Rachel. "Well, what are we to do?"

"Henry Bouvier got to have operate."

"Right now?"

"Yes, she's dying."

Rigger blinked. Building a dollhouse of cushions was what he'd expected. "Who'll do the surgery?"

She looked at him, her brows knitted as well as a four-year-old can do that sort of thing.

"Operate," he explained. "Who's going to operate on her?"

"You are," she said matter-of-factly, as if that should have been obvious. "But first she has to go to the bathroom."

"Wolf is in the upstairs bathroom, but there's another one, just down that hall." He pointed toward a hallway to the right of the fireplace.

Rachel looked intently into Henry's eyes. A small volume of two-way optical twittering went on for several seconds.

"Nope," Rachel said, "has to be the upstairs bathroom."

"Okay, but—"

The girl jumped up and ran toward the stairs, giving the kitchen a quick look.

"Hey," Rigger said in a loud whisper.

She stopped, turning toward him, her foot on the second step.

"You forgot Henry." He picked up the doll from where she lay at his feet.

Rachel ran back, grabbed Henry from his hand, and ran again for the stairs. With another glance toward the kitchen, she bounded up the steps.

Rigger smiled. *Wolf—Appearance - 10, Likability - 10, Attitude - 10, Usefulness - 10. Perfect score.*

Five minutes passed. He listened to the too-loud cleaning noises coming from the kitchen. Another five minutes, and Rigger began to wonder if Rachel was all right.

The woman came in from the kitchen, wiping her hands on a towel. "Where's Rachel?"

"Um...in the bathroom." Rigger looked at the stairway, then at the hall. "It's down there." He pointed toward the hall on the right side of the fireplace, where the downstairs bathroom was.

"Well, I probably need to do that next anyway." She started for the hall.

"Wait!"

She stopped and stared at him.

"How did you do in the kitchen?" He went to inspect her work. She followed.

"Oh, man," she mumbled loud enough for him to hear. "I hope this isn't going to be one of those kind of jobs."

After a cursory inspection of the kitchen, he glanced over the woman's right shoulder, watching the stairway. "Looks pretty good."

Her face took on a quizzical expression.

"I'm sorry," he said. "I never asked your name."

"Katrina. Katrina Raider."

He held out his hand to her. She took it. Her hand was limp and cold in his. He let go.

"I'm Rigger."

"Glad to meet you. How many bedrooms you got in this place?"

He regarded her, wondering why she asked that.

"It's a professional question. I've got to clean them, you know."

"Oh. Three."

"You sleep in all of them?"

Rigger knew this wasn't a joke. "Yes." He saw Rachel tiptoeing down the stairs with Henry and smiled. "But not every night." He waited until the girl took a seat on the hearth. "Come on, I'll show you where they are."

"Hi, Mama," Katrina said as she and Rigger walked into the living room. "What'cha been doing?"

Rigger marveled at how sweet she was to the girl and contrasted that wonderful camaraderie he saw between them with the resentful, almost spiteful way Katrina talked to him. He envied a relationship so close, a mother and her little girl could call each other 'Mama.'

"Thinking," Rachel said.

"About what?"

"That house with a yard back grass you told about."

"You mean grass back yard."

"And monkey box."

"Monkey bars."

"And sand box."

"Is that your gadget?" Katrina asked Rigger, nodding toward the mantel.

Rigger looked at it, then back at her. "Excuse me?"

"I said, what is that gadget?"

He walked to the fireplace and reached for the object. It was an electromechanical device suspended in a solid block of clear Lucite. It measured exactly three and a half inches square. He rotated it to catch the light, admiring the precision milled parts and tiny gold-etched circuit paths running zig-zags over the octagonal silver cover.

"It's a triple-stabilized, self-calibrating thermionic

gyroscope."

"Oh." She took it from his outstretched hand. "Sounds dangerous."

"Only if you hold it too close to your heart." He grinned at her.

She held it away from her body and looked at the other side. "What's it for?"

"It's part of the guidance system for cruise missiles."

"Really?"

"Yes." He expected some show of admiration, or at least approval.

"Then you've killed a lot of people." She handed it back to him.

"Maybe I should've said it's used in the guidance system of the Benedict Arnold also." He put the gyroscope back on the mantel. "Or at least a variation of this one."

"Traitor?" she said. "The anti-cruise-missile missile?"

He raised an eyebrow.

"I'm destitute, not illiterate. There was an exhaustive article in Newsweek last month about the Benedict Arnold, also known as The Traitor."

Rigger had read the same article. During the second Gulf War, eight cruise missiles had gone astray, three of them killing civilians. The same problem had occurred in the Afghanistan war. It was during that war the Pentagon decided to proceed with development of the Benedict Arnold, which soon became called the Traitor. Its main purpose was to birddog the Navy's Tomahawk cruise missiles. If one of them deviated from its course, even by as little as two degrees, the Traitor, which measured less than four feet in length, would instantly accelerate and destroy the errant cruise missile. Still an embarrassing mistake, having a highly developed weapon misbehave, but an airburst wasn't nearly as deadly as having a confused cruiser fly through the window of a new bride's wedding party. If the cruise missile performed as prescribed, then the Traitor would follow it into the target and add its own small contribution to the resultant explosion.

The second reason the guys in the Pentagon E-Ring wanted the Traitor developed was for use against enemy cruise missiles. This was, perhaps, the more important mission; a mission they knew would play a leading role in next war.

"Where's your copy of the gyro for the Traitor?" she asked.

"They wouldn't let me have one." He didn't bother to add that the new model was still too hush-hush even for the developer to have one in his own home. There was also the Dragonfly project, but he felt no desire to invite any more animosity from her; she was hostile enough.

"Now I'm impressed," the woman said.

Rigger stared at her for a moment, thinking it would have felt better if she'd simply slapped his face. "I'll show you the bedrooms."

The words came out with a flinty edge, leaving a bitter taste in his mouth. He walked past her toward the hallway. He'd had enough of her surly attitude. After showing her the master bedroom downstairs and two additional bedrooms upstairs, he left her and returned to the living room to find the little girl.

"What's your name?" Rachel asked.

"Rigger Entime."

She held Henry in front of her face, with the doll facing Rigger. "I don't think so," she said in her deepest voice.

"Then what do you think my name is?"

"God." She laid Henry on the carpet and began removing the doll's clothing.

Rigger was taken aback. *God?* he thought. *A god is a creator; not a destroyer. Obviously, she doesn't realize who God is, or isn't.*

"Well, Rachel..." He was lost for a moment. "I've been mistaken for a lot of different people, but never anyone as magnanimous as He."

She looked up at him, narrowing her eyes. She then crooked her pointer finger, motioning him to come closer.

He bent down.

"There's something I have to tell you," she whispered.

"What's that?" he whispered, too.

"I don't like big words."

He straightened up. "Oh, sorry."

"If you're going to use big words, you have to talk to Kat...I mean Mama." She went back to work on Henry. "She knows about big words."

"Well, I'd much rather talk to you." *Rachel—Appearance - 10, Likability - 10, Attitude - 9, Usefulness - 7.*

"I think it's right here," she said. Henry lay naked on the floor between them, smiling up at Rigger. Rachel pressed her fingertip to the doll's tummy.

"What's right there?"

The little girl jumped up and ran toward the hallway, then down the hall to where Katrina worked in the bathroom. A moment later, she came running back and fell to her knees at the doll's side.

"Apengitus," she said.

"Apengitus?" He stifled a chuckle. "You mean appendicitis?"

"Yes, and it's got to come out."

Rigger went to the kitchen and came back with an assortment of flatware and three linen napkins. He laid out forks, spoons, and a butter knife beside the ailing Barbie doll.

Rachel stared up at him, her eyes wide.

"It's okay," Rigger reassured her as he knelt on the floor. "Henry won't feel a thing. Now, I'll be the doctor, and you'll be the nurse. When I ask for an instrument—"

She gave him a severe look.

"I mean tool. When I ask for a tool, you'll hand me one of those." He took one of the white linen napkins, folded it twice, and placed it over Henry's face. "Now she's out. We can get to work." He flipped a second napkin into a triangle and tied it around his face, outlaw mask fashion. He placed the third napkin around Rachel's face in the same manner, tying it in the back.

Rachel took her place on the opposite side of Henry, glancing from Rigger to the doll.

"Butter knife," he said, holding out his hand to Rachel as he pressed an index finger to the doll's stomach.

* * * * *

Ten minutes later the operation was over, the offending appendix removed, and Henry still slept under the napkin.

Rachel and Rigger looked up to find Katrina staring at the two masked operators on either side of a naked doll, with a collection of silverware lying around. The doll's face was still covered.

"We did it," Rachel cried as she pulled down her mask and whipped the napkin off Henry's face, then grabbed the doll. "Her belly's fixed, and pretty soon she'll be able to dance the ballet again. God said so."

29

"Really?" Katrina said. "Ballet?"

For the first time, Rigger saw the tiniest smile soften her face.

Rachel dressed Henry as Rigger gathered up the flatware. He pulled down his mask as he got up, leaving it to hang around his neck. He walked toward the kitchen.

Katrina followed. "I'm finished, except for that one room upstairs. You'll have to unlock the door if you want it cleaned."

"No, it's fine." He dropped the silverware into the sink and thought about the Dragonfly behind that locked door.

"Guess you wanna inspect everything."

Rigger faced her. "No, but I need your phone number."

"Why?"

"You do such good work, I may want you again."

As they walked back to the living room, he jotted down the phone number she gave him.

"Come on, Rach, we've got to go now."

As soon as Rigger saw them out, he picked up the phone to make a call. When someone answered on the other end, he said, "Hi, Pugsley." He listened for a moment. "Yeah, I'm fine." He pulled the mask from around his neck to daub at his forehead, while the other man talked. "Listen," Rigger interrupted him and glanced down at the notepad with Katrina's phone number. "I've got a job for you."

Chapter Four

Rigger didn't die on that night, almost a year before, but something went wrong inside his body. In that bloody parking lot, he picked up some dreadful disease, perhaps something those two deviants left on the ground or in the air. Some alien pathogen that crept into him as he stood looking down at what was left of his life. A timed-release murder, relentlessly gnawing at his insides, destroying him from within.

He didn't actually know where the disease came from, but in his seething rage at what those two had done to his life, he imagined they were killing him as well.

Ten months passed before he realized or even cared that something was wrong with him. His doctor put him through an exhaustive battery of tests, taking almost a week. The day he met Katrina and Rachel on the street was the day he'd received his death sentence. On previous visits to Dr. Ruth Macintyre's clinic, her nurses had drawn blood and taken other samples from him. They sent them off to some laboratory for analysis. They ran EKGs, EEGs, CAT scans, stress tests—the works. Later came more blood and urine analysis. Then on that fateful day, his doctor delivered the dreaded news.

"Spongiform encephalopathy," she told him.

After a half-hour of sitting beside him on her Sears couch, holding his hand, and going into great detail about current research, online support groups, and hope for patients in the future, she told him the hard truth.

"Rigger, in all my years of practice, I've never had to tell a patient there's no hope. There's always been an array of drugs, surgeries, and other treatments, radiation, chemotherapy for me to choose from. But this time, there's nothing for me to cut out, there's no tumor to bombard with radiation, and no infection to fight with drugs." Dr. Macintyre let go of his hand and stood up to pace the floor before him. "It's an insidious disease that worms its way into the cerebellum and bores tentacles into every corner of the brain. I'm sorry, Rigger; it's inoperable, incurable. Go home and make peace with your God or get roaring drunk, it's your choice."

She gave him a yellow plastic bag filled with sample vials of Buprenorphine, a narcotic analgesic and powerful painkiller. She also wrote a prescription for morphine, refillable without limit, an anti-depressant, and Nexium and Tagamet to combat the side effects of the other medications.

Yes, he said in answer to her suggestion, he would get a second opinion, and a third. But he knew his days were numbered. He'd be dead in less than a year, according to Dr. Macintyre.

* * * * *

The ringing of the phone jolted Rigger from his soft recliner. The sun was up, but the room cowered in darkness, as if fearful of the new day.

"Hey, Rig." Pugsley's voice came from the receiver. "That phone number you gave me to check on? It's a home for battered women."

"What?"

"Yeah, but you can't talk to anyone. They have a

series of voicemail boxes where you leave a message. If the woman wants to talk to you, she'll call you back."

"Pugsley, that's all you got?"

"There ain't nothing to get; it's a dead end."

"Even a dove leaves a trail through the mist, if one has the eye to see it."

"Yeah, well, that may have worked for Longfellow and Hiawatha, but I gotta have feathers. You got Caller ID, right?"

"Yes."

"Then call that place, leave a message for her, and my bet is, she'll call back from a different number. That's the trail of your little bird I need to see."

* * * * *

Rigger called Pugsley the next day. He'd dialed the number Katrina gave him and left a message, saying he wanted her to come back the following week to clean his apartment. She'd called back an hour later and told him she'd be there on Tuesday.

"Anonymous," he told Pugsley over the phone as he looked at the display on his Caller ID.

"Great!"

"Great?" Rigger said. "What's so great about anonymous?"

"Have you received any other calls?"

"No, she called just a minute ago."

"Then pull the plug on your phone line. I'll be right over."

Ten minutes later when Pugsley knocked, Wolf beat Rigger to the door, yipping with puppy excitement. As soon as Pugsley stepped inside, Wolf attacked and gnawed a shoestring on a shiny cordovan Oxford.

Pugsley picked up the dog. "Now, this," he said as he ruffled the blond and tan hair on the puppy's head, "is a good idea." The little dog squirmed and licked his hand. "You need something lively in this place."

"I guess so." Rigger smiled. "Too bad he can't learn to use a litter box."

"How you feeling these days?"

"Better, thanks."

"Yeah," Pugsley said softly. His face hardened into a severe expression. "I can see that."

Rigger brought Pugsley a cup of coffee as he wired a homemade electronic device between Rigger's Caller ID and phone line.

"Two creams, two sugars." Rigger placed the cup on the end table, by the phone. "Right?"

"Yeah, Rig. Thanks." He took a sip, smacked his lips. "Perfect. Sweet and smooth." He set down the cup. "Now," he said, rubbing his hands together, "first we set your phone to 'Anonymous.'" He pushed some buttons on his device. "Then we page back on your Caller ID." Pressing the back button on Rigger's Caller ID brought up the Anonymous entry from Katrina's call. "Now we do magic."

He pressed a button, but nothing happened. Pugsley checked the connections on his box, then on the phone. He laughed when he found the phone was still unplugged from the wall.

Slipping the phone cable into the wall plug, he pressed a button on his device, and they heard the rapid tones of a number being dialed. After a few seconds, they heard sounds of relay clicks at the phone company's substation, and a second number was dialed. As soon as it rang one time, a phone number popped up on the red digital display of Pugsley's device. He flipped a switch to disconnect the call.

"If she has Caller ID," he said, "all she'll see is 'Anonymous' on her end." He took out a small notepad and his pen. "That's a different number, right?"

Rigger glanced at the number on the display. "Yes, it is."

"This little box is more fun that a windy day on the Street of Short Skirts." Pugsley removed his electronic device and reconnected Rigger's Caller ID. Five minutes later, his coffee finished, he was out the front door on his way to resume digging.

Pugsley—Appearance - 2, Likability - 10, Attitude - 10, Usefulness - 10.

* * * * *

Two hours later, Rigger got a call from Pugsley.

"Katrina Loraine Raider, twenty-three-oh-one Kimberley Ridge, Number twenty-one, a townhouse, thirty-two hundred bucks a month is the rent—"

Rigger interrupted him. "What the Sam Hill are you talking about? She lives on the street."

"Twenty-six years old, five-foot-four, dark hair, dark eyes. That sound like your dove?"

"Yes, but—"

"Last month's electric bill, three-hundred-eighty-two, water and trash, forty-seven, both paid on time, employed at Wellington Labs—"

"Employed?"

"Works the swing shift, six p.m. till two a.m."

"I can't believe all this nonsense."

"She has a degree in—get this—pharmacological ethnobotany. I know you're going to tell me what that is."

"It's the study of how cultural groups use indigenous plants to make medicine."

"Well, why the hell don't they just say that?"

"Wouldn't look good on a diploma."

"Right," Pugsley said. "She's also going to school part-time, working on her master's degree."

Rigger was quiet, trying to assimilate all this alien information about a street woman he thought he knew.

"Drives a late model Volvo, dark red, never married—"

"Pugsley, what's going on here? When I met this woman, she and her daughter were begging on the street."

"Daughter?"

"Yeah, she has a four-year-old girl."

"Nope. This babe has no dependents."

"Pug, my friend, I've wondered when you'd screw up and get tangled in the wiring of that computer of yours." Rigger was relieved in a way. He knew he couldn't be that far off on Katrina. "Admit it, you struck out on this one."

"I doubt that. What's the kid's name?"

"Rachel. And her doll's name is Henry Bulyea." Rigger chuckled. "Maybe you can track down something on her."

"Her who?"

"The doll, Henry."

"Her doll's name is Henry?"

"Yeah, a Barbie doll named Henry Bulyea. I bet there's lots of info on the Internet about her."

"How you spelling that last name?"

Rigger spelled it out.

"I'll call you back."

The line clicked as Pugsley hung up.

* * * * *

No dependents, Rigger thought as he hurried down the

36

street. He checked his watch again. *Pugsley tracked down the wrong woman; that's the only explanation. Miswired that little box of his, that's what happened. Dialed the wrong number.*

At 12:29, he sat at the bus stop across the street from Miss Wiggley's Day Care. At 12:30, it seemed as if a large school bus had been tipped up to spill a load of laughing kids into the play yard. Rigger leaned forward, intent on the children–especially the girls, one little girl in particular. It wasn't Rachel, but like Rachel, she had a flouncy air about her, that little loose-limbed, almost awkward stride, and there was a musical note in her laughter that he knew so well. She could have been Rachel's sister.

Thirty minutes later, Rigger, empty of purpose and bereft of hope, trudged home, keeping to the edge of the cold afternoon shadows.

Halfway home, in the middle of the block, on a nearly deserted side street, he stopped.

This is creepy. I've heard of people feeling someone's eyes watching them from behind, but I always thought it a bit melodramatic.

He turned quickly and saw someone. He couldn't tell if it was a man or woman. The person jumped into a doorway. Curious, he walked back. When he came to the doorway, he found it led into a place called O'Malley's Bar and Grill. The glass-half of the door was grimy and frosted around the edges. In the dim interior, he made out a dozen or so patrons sitting at the bar, sipping their drinks. Three more sat at a beat-up wooden table, playing dominos. They were all men, and it could have been any one of them.

Chapter Five

Rigger's besieged mind played tricks on him. At times, he imagined the tentacles of his disease reached slimy fingers into a synapse of his brain circuitry and tapped out some coded message to disrupt and bewilder his engineer's logical sense of reason. Occasionally, these episodes would deliver a brilliant and painful burst of lightning. At other times, his mind would fill with boiling, silent thunderheads. Today, it was nothing more than a thick gray mist, echoing a persistent ringing. No matter what the mental weather, his intellect swung from near-genius to something either side of imbecile and back again.

Finally, he struggled to his feet to answer the ringing doorbell. An apple, wet-cherry red and glowing with a juicy crunch of promise, seemed to float of its own accord toward him. Rigger glanced from the apple to Katrina's smile as she and Rachel stood at his opened door. Katrina held out the apple to him.

An offering? An offering of what?

His mind jumped to that well-known image of Adam and Eve, with the plucked apple between them. Within the span of a few voracious heartbeats, the apple core dropped to the virgin Eden grass, followed by two heavenly bodies, and innocence evaporated into the primordial mist.

At this late date, well beyond the age of enlightenment, things aren't always as they seem. But Rigger didn't care. Metaphors and motives could go unanalyzed forever, or go to the movies or to the blazes, as far as he was concerned.

He took the apple from Katrina's moist palm and felt a delicate, revealing warmth, a few degrees above his own. With Wolf held snugly in the crook of his arm—to dampen the dog's excitement, but also give him something to cling to—Rigger swung the door wide and waved the ladies in, with a flourished salaam.

One female, small, smiling, and sweet, an enormous vacuum waiting to be filled with music and laughter. The other, a beautiful enigma, closed to all who would try to steal a glimpse of her hidden secrets. And yet that translucent mask seemed to pale in the glow of familial tenderness radiating from the man and little girl.

Other than a microscopic layer of dust, not easily seen except by one or two afternoon sunbeams slanting through a zebraed west window, the apartment was as neat and clean as Katrina left it the week before.

"Know what we should do?" he asked.

Katrina, Rachel, Henry and Wolf looked at Rigger with a mixture of feigned boredom and keen anticipation.

"To heck with cleaning this place. Let's take this apple to the park and make a picnic of it."

And so, in the late morning on the thirteenth of January, the sun warmed Rigger and Katrina as they sat on a sculptured boulder-bench in Central Park and watched a budding love affair between a laughing girl and furry frolicker of mixed heritage. Wolf with his new red collar, and Rachel with mismatched shoes—one a little blue untied sneaker, the other a pink ballet slipper. She didn't care about fashion, and apparently the dog didn't either. They ran, jumped, and tumbled, laughing and barking all the while.

"How old is he?"

"What?" Rigger asked. Sometimes Katrina yanked him back from his musings so violently, it was almost annoying.

"The puppy," she said. "How old?"

"Oh, two months, I think."

"And what will happen to him?"

"When?"

"When you..." She stopped and started over. "When you grow tired of him. When you're sick of taking him outside twice a day, every day. When you decide you're going to give yourself a little vacation and you want to be rid of him. What will you do?"

"I guess I'll find a home for him before I go."

"In ten years, he'll be old," she said. "In fourteen years, he'll be dead. It seems selfish and cruel to me, to make someone love you and then die."

"He doesn't know he's going to die someday. And I doubt he's trying to make anyone love him. He's only trying to enjoy what little bit of life he has."

"What if he knew he was going to die?" she asked.

"So? If he knew death was near, do you think he should just go off into the woods so he wouldn't accidentally cause some misguided fool to fall in love with him?" Rigger turned at the sound of Rachel's squeal as Wolf growled and tugged at Henry's dress. "Is that your philosophy?"

"I guess I don't have any philosophy. I only have feelings and intuition. But I know what I want to do before

I die."

"What's that?"He gazed into the deep brown of her eyes.

"Do you know what a pharmacopeia is?" She held his steady gaze.

"Yes, but I think that's been done."

"Not for all the indigenous tribes."

"All…" *Damn it, Pugsley.*

Rigger looked down at the ground, where a drove of ants dismembered a green and black beetle. The poor devil squirmed and wriggled his three remaining legs. His mouth parts moved erratically, emitting some silent insect scream. A fat toad sat on a stone nearby, surrounded by graceful dead reeds, overseeing the demise of the beetle with a judge's stoic impartiality. The warty amphibian eyed the doomed defendant with cold boredom.

Damn it all to hell, Pugsley—why do you always have to be right?

"Well, not all the tribes," she said. "I'd like to do just one."

"We're hungry," Rachel cried as she and the pup ran toward them. "Can we have brown milk and cookiecake at that place we like to go?"

The four of them left the park for Hannibal's Café.

Formica pratensis, a young pissant, no larger than a dream bud suspended upon the crest of a distant horizon, clung to the precipice of the stone boulder-bench and peered over.

He gazed up in wide-eyed amazement at the enormous apple core towering above and marveled at his good fortune as he rubbed his feathered antennae together.

* * * * *

"Hi there, Rig, ole buddy. How you doing?"

"You sound rather chipper this morning, Pugsley." It was just after eight in the morning. Rigger had picked up the phone on the first ring, thinking it was someone else.

"Yep, and you're gonna owe me a dinner if I got this one right."

"Well, if not, I'll still treat you to a Whopper."

"Could that Barbie doll's name be Henry Bouvier?" He spelled Bouvier.

"Might be. Sounds like Bulyea."

"Listen to this. Rachel Bouvier Henry. Age four years, two months. Blonde hair, sky blue eyes. Am I close?"

"Yes."

"Are you sitting down?"

"I am now."

"Residence, for the past six months, twenty-three eighteen East forty-fifth." Pugsley paused.

"And? Come on, Pug, you've squeezed all you're gonna get out of this."

"That, my friend, is the address of St. Cecilia's Orphanage."

* * * * *

Too late for love. Time now only for a brief infatuation.

Katrina was right about it being a cruel joke to make someone love you and then die. Rigger knew Rachel had begun to bond with him, and he wanted desperately to be a father again, even if only for a year.

Is that so heartless? She could use a father, someone to hold her close, take her to the zoo...let her have the freedom of littlegirlhood.

But after a year, then what? And his last months, he knew, would be ugly and painful. She wouldn't have a stand-in father then; only a dying invalid on her hands. And when he was gone, would she be sad, melancholy, grief-stricken? Or would she rebound quickly, as children sometimes do, and find another father?

No, it's no good. Only my selfish ego taking over.

Plastered up, hammered-tin vanity—that was his leaky armor. Better to love little girls from a distance. Let them run and play in ignorance of his presence. He could hold them in his imagined fatherhood but let them remain free of his coming death and all its hideous trappings.

But what about a deal? Everything up front. I have eight or nine months of some sort of imitation life remaining. Make them a bargain. They can stay with me for nine months, then I'm off on a...a what? A research trip. The Middle East, looking for some forgotten monarch's tomb. Or to the mountains of Mexico to track the elusive and vicious Monarch butterfly to its wintertime lair. People disappear in the East all the time, and even in the West. I could just go into the desert woods and slowly disappear from Rachel's memory. She would have Wolf, they could run and play in the sunshine for many years. A four-year-old's memory is soft and reusable. After a while, she'd ask Katrina, "Who was that old man we used to live with? He was funny sometimes. Can you remember his name?"

Rigger; Appearance - 7, Likability - 2, Attitude - 0, Usefulness - 0.

* * * * *

Pugsley's misaligned nose and one cauliflower ear, along with a slightly offset lower jaw, were mementos of his boxing days. One might think his appearance more attractive to a bulldog bitch than a woman, but such wasn't the case.

His quick smile and athletic build, along with his little-boy hair style and disarming way of brushing off his street-scarred appearance, easily won over women. Not always in a romantic way, but certainly in a conversational, group get-together sort of way. He didn't know a lot about any one subject, but he was knowledgeable in many different areas. This facet of his personality gave him the ability to talk to anyone about almost any subject, and he always displayed an eagerness to gain insight into new areas.

Since most people enjoy talking about their particular area of expertise, he continually added to his store of knowledge, and in the process engendered relationships leading to untapped sources of useful information.

Pugsley, at thirty-two, was a professional digger and hacker. On contract to a dozen private investigators and, usually off the record, several police detectives. He kept very busy.

The police work he performed not for money, but rather for "tokens of exchange." These tokens he accumulated and cashed in when in need of a bit of data about a crime or some perpetrator in detention. The detectives were only too happy to give him what they could, because his resources went far beyond what they were legally allowed to do.

He never engaged in any illegal activities, but neither was he restricted by the bureaucratic restrictions of search warrants and court orders or artificial boundaries of political or diplomatic privilege. He stretched the definition of "illegal" when he dealt with people living outside the law. For example, in the term "breaking and entering," the word "breaking" didn't apply to him, in his opinion, if number one, the home or automobile he wanted to enter was owned or controlled by a known criminal, and number two, he had in his possession a key or reasonable facsimile thereof.

His theory was, any information left unguarded was his to borrow, as long as he left the original untainted.

There was something else about Pugsley—he never allowed his friends to burrow too deeply into depression or self-imposed pity states. If one was suffering from a broken relationship or the loss of a family member, or perhaps a serious illness, Pugsley wouldn't withdraw from that friendship. He would instead impose himself more strongly than normal to distract the sufferer into new channels of activity, even when that person preferred to be left alone.

On this particular day, having come in from a sunny morning, he seemed to bring a bit of it along with him into Rigger's apartment, brightening an otherwise gloomy home.

They sat in the kitchen with coffee and cinnamon rolls, talking first of nature and geography, then of insects. Rigger was an engineer, but he was also a parataxonomist—an amateur who searches for new species of living creatures. He was keenly interested in finding the smallest insect capable of flight.

"There's some lower limit," Rigger said, "probably microscopic, where wing surface is ineffective against the molecules of air. But just above that level, there might exist an insect never before identified. I'd like to find that little critter."

They talked for a while about what part of the world might likely be home to this tiny insect. Probably the Amazon, they decided. Pugsley then got around to the reason for his visit.

"I got some sad news. But first, let me tell you this. You can do a positive ID on the little girl. She should have a three-inch scar somewhere on her left side, below the rib cage. If you get a chance, check on that. I'm pretty sure you'll find it there."

"Right," Rigger said. "I'll just tell a four-year-old girl to take her clothes off for me."

"Well, you can do it that way, but I would be a little more subtle."

"Oh, sure. Hey, Rachel, I think you need a bath."

"No. Try using the doll. Come on, Rig, you have some imagination left."

"All right, Pug. I'll figure something out. Now, what's the sad news? Like I haven't heard any for a while."

Pugsley gave his friend a severe look. "In a minute. First, there's something else."

"What's that?" Rigger asked.

"I need a key."

"For what?"

"Your front door. There's going to come a time when I might..." He paused, sipping his coffee. "I might need to get in."

Rigger squeezed his eyes shut. Pug, the realist. He knew there would come a time when Rigger wouldn't be able to answer the door. Dr. Macintyre told him he was dying, and now his best friend just told him the same thing. Hope escaped in a stampede over the horizon, along with youth, love, and all the other positive aspects of life. It would be a lonely downhill now, down the mountainside into that well-known valley of no return.

"All right," Rigger whispered. "I have a spare one you can have." He swallowed and took a deep breath. "Now, give me the rest of it."

"Rachel's parents were murdered in a mall parking

lot. Little over six months ago, butchered, the kid saw the whole thing, she got cut herself. Some little old lady in an SUV came roaring up in the middle of the crime, horn blaring, jumped out with an enormous three-fifty-seven Magnum, and the killers ran for the hills. She put two slugs in their departing tailgate. If not for the lady and her pistol, the girl would be dead, too."

"Good Lord! The poor child."

"Yeah, in fact, after a few days, when she stopped screaming, she was able to give an iffy description of the perps."

It was a long time before Rigger spoke. "You said Katrina works in some sort of lab."

"Yes, Wellington Labs."

"Find out exactly what her duties are." Rigger drank the last bit of his coffee and stood to put the cup in the sink. He stared out the kitchen window for a moment. "I've got a hunch about her and what she does at that lab."

Chapter Six

When Autumn parked the B-17 in front of the airport terminal at Rio, Anderson jumped out with a pair of yellow wooden blocks. He was followed by Matthew, carrying a second set of blocks. They ran to wedge them in front of and behind the wheels of the main landing gear.

Anderson walked out in front of the aircraft, to where Autumn could see him. He held his hand up, palm toward her, and she knew he wanted her to idle the engines for a moment before shutting down.

Anderson glanced at the feathered starboard inboard engine, then went to stand before the outboard engine. He listened for a moment, then hurried to the other side of the plane. Autumn and her grandfather watched him pause before the port side inboard engine before going to the fourth and final engine.

He cocked his head and stood for more than a minute, listening. Finally, he looked toward Autumn and lifted his hands over his head. He crossed his wrists and slowly brought down his arms.

Autumn shut down the three engines and flipped off the fuel pump switches.

"What's up with number four?" she asked her grandfather.

"If there's anything wrong, you can bet Anderson heard it. He'll let us know if it's got a major problem. All four engines are about due for an overhaul. Maybe after New York, we'll cancel the rest of the tour and head for Virginia to put the Shenandoah in the hangar. The boys can have her for a month or two."

"I'm sure going to miss this old war horse when I go back to school next month."

"This old war horse is going to miss you, too. You want to fly the Cessna to MIT?"

"Yes, if it's okay with you."

"Sure. A plane's no good to anybody sitting on the ground."

"Looks like a couple hundred people today," Autumn said as they worked through their post-landing checklist.

Her grandfather looked at the crowd behind the ropes and nodded. "Even in Brazil, they like to come out to see our old bomber."

Five airport security guards posted themselves at intervals along the rope to keep the sightseers at bay until the crew was ready for them.

Ten minutes later, Autumn put away the completed checklist and ruffled her flaming red hair. She took her garrison cap from the back of the seat, put it on, and adjusted it to a rakish angle. She flipped her long hair back over her shoulder, then looked at her grandfather.

"How's that?"

He put on his own cap and tilted it to match hers. "Perfect."

She reached to fix his collar, then stood and squeezed out between the two seats. It felt good to be standing after four and a half hours in the cramped cockpit. She stretched and looked around for Matthew but saw he was already outside. When she got down to the open door in the belly of the plane, she waited for Grandfather Willow.

"After you, Skipper," she said when he stood beside her.

"Uh-uh. The pilot goes out first."

She gave him a smile, then knelt down to grip the edge of the doorway and swung herself to the tarmac below. When she stepped out from under the plane and straightened her leather jacket, she saw the four crewmen standing in a line to her left, at parade rest.

She, along with the men in the crew, wore authentic military uniforms from the World War II era, including Eighth Air Force arm patches and an insignia shield on their left breasts, featuring the Shenandoah on a bombing raid.

As soon as her grandfather dropped to the ground behind Autumn, Anderson called out "Atten-SHUN," from his place at the end of the line, and all four men came to attention.

The crowd applauded as she walked before the men, followed by her grandfather. Anderson popped a snappy salute when Autumn passed by. She watched them with a critical eye, as if in review. The second man from the end crossed his eyes and stuck his tongue out the side of his mouth.

"Shut up, Matthew," she whispered, then turned toward the rope to shake hands and see if anyone wanted to go inside of the Shenandoah.

* * * * *

Two days later, the B-17 winged north, high above the Amazon. Grandpa Willow was at the controls, while Autumn unfolded a flying chart.

She studied the map for a moment and pressed the button on the intercom. "How long, Matthew?"

"Two and a half minutes, if that airspeed you gave me is right this time."

She glanced at the airspeed indicator. "Two-twenty knots, and yes, it's right."

"It wasn't right when we arrived at Manaus forty-five minutes late."

"Andrews fixed it."

"That's what worries me."

"Just give us a heads-up when we get close."

"Aye-aye, Sir Madam."

She clicked the button twice and smiled to herself. Matthew sat in the navigator's seat just behind her, and she knew he was smiling.

Two minutes later, he came on the intercom. "Thirty seconds."

Autumn looked out her side window and studied the ground, ten thousand feet below. The green canopy of the Amazon Basin stretched from horizon to horizon, broken only by two columns of smoke rising from the rainforest some fifty miles to the east.

Ten million creatures, maybe more, within my field of vision. From microscopic insects at the bottom of the food chain to the mighty jaguar at the top, millions of flying, climbing, slithering creatures, and I can't see a single one from up here.

"Fascinating," Grandpa Willow broke into her revelry. "Isn't it?"

Autumn turned from the side window and looked out over the nose of the plane, seeing nothing but the green of the rainforest and blue sky. She then leaned forward to look past her grandfather and saw the snow-covered peaks of the Andes mountain range, far to the west.

"When I was a kid," she said, "and studied the globe in your office, I always thought someone flying over the equator would see a wide yellow band going around the Earth. But here we are, going from the Southern Hemisphere into the Northern, leaving summer behind and flying into winter, and nothing has changed."

"I know. You'd think at least the compass would take a wild swing or we'd hit an air pocket and get bumped around, or the sky would go to a darker shade of blue. But nothing has changed, except we're closer to home."

"We'll see a big change by Wednesday. Matthew said there's a snowstorm blowing into New York City."

"Great," he said. "I love snow."

"Yeah, but you don't like it on the runway."

"JFK does a good job with snow removal. It'll be clear long before we get there."

"Will we ever come this way again?" She tucked the folded flying chart into the map case and looked back to the hazy horizon.

"I won't." He was silent for a moment. "But you might."

"Five seconds," Matthew's voice came over the intercom. "Three, two, one. Bling. Welcome to the northern half of the world."

Chapter Seven

Rigger attached the leash to Wolf's collar, and the puppy lunged for the front door, knowing it was time for his morning walk.

"Hang on, pal." Rigger let go of the leash and went to the hall closet. "You've got your coat on, but I don't have mine yet."

The puppy ran from the front door to the closet, then sat yipping at Rigger's feet. When the closet door opened, the dog rushed inside but came out right away, then ran back to the front door.

"Don't you know there's a blizzard out there?"

Rigger put on his heavy overcoat, tied a wool scarf around his neck, then pulled a black stocking cap down over his ears. After buckling up his boots and patting his coat pocket to be sure his gloves were there, he was ready to go.

Once outside, Rigger and Wolf headed for Central Park, just a block away.

Wolf bounded along, pulling Rigger through the gusting wind. The snow fell heavily, and the wind whipped it into drifts at every turn of the trail.

When they returned to the apartment building, they met a man in the foyer with his tiny Chihuahua.

"You're not taking Esperanza out in this weather, are you, Mr. Greer?" Rigger asked as he stomped the snow from his boots and reached to shake hands with the old veteran.

"Of course. She loves it, and so do I."

Rigger watched Mr. Greer wrap a yellow and red knitted scarf around his neck. The history of the old man's most recent three meals could be clearly traced down the front to his pea-green shirt.

"But we've got a gale blowing outside," Rigger said. "With snow drifting up to Esperanza's ears."

"Great!" Mr. Greer zipped up his insulated jacket and buttoned his long, gray overcoat. "That's what I love about New York City. We get all kinds of weather. From sweltering heat to freezing blizzards. Just think how boring it would be to live in Hawaii, where my Edna wants to live. It's seventy degrees every day, I tell her. And every evening, the same seventy degrees. There's the same blue sky every day and the same rain shower at four every afternoon. Weathermen can't even get a job there, for Christ's sake. People don't even talk about the weather in Hawaii. What's there to talk about? It's the same tomorrow, next week, next month for crying out loud. But here, in beautiful NYC, we got ourselves a roaring blizzard."

Rigger glanced down at the little short-haired Chihuahua in her pink knitted vest. She shivered and turned her large, sad eyes up to Rigger, as if imploring him to save her from this mad man who wanted her to relieve herself outside in the ice and snow. Rigger gave her an understanding tilt of his head but then shrugged as if he were helpless against her master.

Esperanza licked her nose and looked back at the elevator door, perhaps calculating her odds at making a run for it and peeing in the corner.

"I just hope this stuff blows out of here by Wednesday," Mr. Greer said, tugging Esperanza back to his feet.

"What's Wednesday?"

"There's a B-17 flying into JFK."

"Really? A B-17 bomber?"

"Yeah," Mr. Greer said. "I was a waist gunner on a B-17 in World War Two. Didn't I ever tell you about that?"

"Yes, I believe you mentioned it once or twice." Rigger admired the man's positive attitude. Even though an insurance company's actuary would probably place a negative value on his remaining life, he took on the new day with eager anticipation.

Rigger wondered about himself. How did others perceive him? Since he knew his days were numbered, did he wear his doom like some sort of badge of honor?

"Hey, look, I'm dying. How about a little sympathy?" Is that how I come across to the people I encounter? Does Rachel sense something wrong with me? And what about Katrina?

Other than his doctor, Pugsley was the only person who knew he was dying. He told Pug because he was aware of Rigger going to the doctor so often. Rigger hadn't told anyone else, but did they see it in his attitude? His changed outlook?

He studied Mr. Greer's untroubled expression as the old man pulled on his fleece-lined leather gloves. His face was etched with age, but unmarred by worry lines. He always seemed ready to smile.

Quality of life. He knows his days are numbered. Maybe he has less time than I do, but he's obviously not moping his final days away. He remains engaged in life, rather than preoccupied with the coming end of it.

With a grin, Mr. Greer touched two fingers to his forehead. "Have a good one."

He pulled open the door, and he and his little dog disappeared into a swirling cloud of blowing snow.

Mr. Greer—Appearance - 8, Likability - 9, Attitude - 10, Usefulness - 10.

Rigger began to whistle "Puff, the Magic Dragon" as he walked toward the elevator. Wolf ran ahead, with his leash trailing on the floor behind him.

The elevator door whooshed open, welcoming him and his dog inside.

"It's time to get back to the Dragonfly," Rigger whispered to his reflection in the mirrored elevator door as he reached to punch the button for the tenth floor.

* * * * *

"Come on, Sarge, can't you give me a peek at that report?"

Pugsley sat beside Sergeant Robolinski's desk. After they'd talked of peripheral affairs and the latest promotions in the department, they discussed the murder of Rachel's parents.

"You know procedures, Pug. No homicide reports, such as file HOM1216, are allowed to leave this department, and no unauthorized access to my computer, where HOM1216 is stored in a folder called HOM-UNSOLVED, will be allowed under any circumstance."

Pugsley grinned. "You talk like a book."

Exotropia was the name of the good sergeant's affliction. He had two wandering eyes, or walleyes. Pugsley was never sure which eye to watch, because as soon as he focused on one, it would wander away to glance at the wall, or out the window, or at the ceiling. The second eye would then take over the duties of regarding the other member of the conversation until, without warning, it would go looking to find what the first eye had sought, and that first eye would come back to fix Pugsley with a severe stare, as if daring him to crack a smile.

Pugsley switched to the man's left eye as the right one drifted away.

Sergeant Robolinski's hand went to his breast pocket, feeling for the pack of Camels. Skinny, with broad shoulders, the 54-year-old officer had sandy red hair. Thick and unruly, it was long past due for a good trim.

"Now," Sarge said. "I'll just be going out on the street for a quick smoke. What happens to my computer while my back is turned, I have no control over, and I can't be responsible for any unauthorized access. Neither God nor Captain Appleby can blame me if some thug sneaks in here and steals something from my computer." He pulled open a drawer and rummaged around through the collection of keys, paper clips, and old ballpoint pens until he found a crumpled scrap of paper, which he smoothed out and laid beside the keyboard of his computer. "I'll be back in five minutes." He left his chair and ambled toward the front door of the police station, the cigarettes and lighter already out of his pocket.

Pugsley looked around to be sure no one paid any attention him, then slipped into the sergeant's chair and clicked the mouse a couple of times. A message popped up, asking for a password. Pugsley looked at the piece of paper Sarge had left by the keyboard and typed in "ANNEKANE." He then took a sixteen-gig flash drive, about the side of his thumbnail, and slipped it into the USB port on the computer.

When the computer chirped, Pugsley looked around, but the other officers went about their business. He surveyed the room and waited for the homicide file to copy to his flash drive. He heard a soft ping and glanced at the screen to see the copy had finished. After removing the flash drive, he returned the computer display to its original position and slipped the piece of paper back into the desk drawer.

"You really need to kick that nasty habit," Pugsley said as he passed Sarge on the front steps of the police station.

The sergeant blew a puff of smoke into the air. "I'm working on it, Pug."

His left eye watched the cloud of gray smoke drift down the street, while the right eye looked after the departing Pugsley.

* * * * *

"Bang!" Rigger cocked his thumb again and pointed with his forefinger. "Bang!" he said. "No, Wolf. You're doing 'beg.'" He laid the dog on the floor, rolled him onto his back, and brushed his palm down the puppy's face so he'd close his eyes. "That's 'bang,' and you play dead. Now, let's do it again."

He'd worked on the Dragonfly all morning, then left it in frustration with his two remaining problems still nagging him—the weak power supply and a clumsy set of makeshift controllers. Wolf was a welcome distraction, and he played with the dog for another half-hour before he went to the kitchen, washed his hands, and made a sandwich. He checked the clock; 1:15. Almost recess time at Tom Thumb's Preschool. Later, he'd go to Heckscher Playground in Central Park, where he liked to have lunch after recess.

He walked the eight blocks to Tom Thumb without Wolf. The puppy was a great kid-magnet, and he knew every child in the preschool's snowy yard would run to play with him as soon as Rigger set him free of his leash. But he also knew it was risky to draw too much attention to himself when he hung around the nurseries and preschools. This time, he clung to the chain-link fence as the children came out to play. He studied the little girls and tried to pick out one who matched his memory.

On that cold, windy afternoon, as he watched a curly blonde, laughing on a swing, he had that eerie feeling again, a feeling of someone behind him. He swung around, but all he saw was snow falling from a shivering cedar shrub at the entrance to a walk-up apartment house, half a block away.

* * * * *

On Friday morning, Rigger let in Pugsley. He seemed to come by often now, seeing Rigger more frequently than in all the years of their friendship.

Pug dropped a thick stack of papers on the table. "That's the police report on the murder of Rachel's parents. I snagged it off Sergeant Robolinski's computer. Something in there you gotta see, but not right now. First, I'll tell you what I found out about Katrina Raider's job."

Rigger looked at the report but left it alone. "What'd you get?"

"She does blood and urine analysis at Wellington Labs." Pugsley stroked the puppy in his lap. The two men sat in the Rigger's study, facing each other across an ancient, intricately carved Ming table.

"Son-of-a-bitch." Rigger slumped in his seat.

Pugsley stopped his hand on the dog's head. "Rig, in the eighteen years I've known you, I've never heard anything stronger than 'damn.' What's got into you?"

"Listen to this, Pug." He sat up, leaning his elbows on his knees, clasping his coffee mug. "A woman works in a lab. She identifies a deadly disease in a man's blood sample. Knows he's dying. Does a little checking, finds out he has no relatives left in the world. Then she borrows a kid from an orphanage, stations herself and the little girl outside the doctor's office on the day she knows he's going to get the bad news." He sipped his coffee, watching Pugsley's reaction.

"Yeah, go on."

"Not once, but twice she posts herself and the kid on the street, where this softhearted jerk is going to see them and feel sorry for two street people, especially the little girl with a stupid cardboard sign hanging around her neck. The woman pretends to have no interest at all in the guy, while letting the girl do all the work. Raider must have coached her for hours. How cunning and diabolical is that?"

"Pretty bad. Guess I've heard worse. But using a kid, an orphan? That's a new low in my book." Pugsley put down his coffee. "What are you going to do about it?"

"Strangle her, torch her red Volvo. Turn her worthless butt over to the police, I don't know."

"No crime done that I can see," Pug said. "Some low-down stuff, but unless Raider kidnapped Rachel, there's no crime committed yet."

* * * * *

Pugsley found the name of the janitorial company doing

cleaning work at Wellington Labs, where Katrina worked.

Rigger went to the company and hired on as a temporary employee. He received a set of uniforms and was told to be ready to report for work the following week, after his background screening report came back.

That evening, Rigger put on one of his new uniforms and parked outside Wellington Labs, waiting until the cleaning crew entered the building. As soon as they were inside, he ran to the front door and told the guard he was sorry about being late for work and to please not tell his supervisor.

The guard told him he better not let it happen again and buzzed him in.

* * * * *

There she was, her back to him, bending over a microscope.

"Hey there," Rigger said, louder than necessary, wanting to startle her.

The woman jumped, apparently unaware anyone else was in the lab. In alarm, she almost unseated herself from the high stool where she sat. After catching her breath, she looked at his uniform; seeing the chest patch of Superior Janitorial Services, she relaxed and gave him a smile.

Rigger didn't smile. His jaw dropped. "I'm s-sorry," he stammered. "Very sorry."

She was about five-foot-four inches tall, slim build, brown hair, brown eyes. Katrina's exact description—except she was also fifty years old, maybe more. At least twice Katrina's age.

He apologized for frightening her. "I thought you were Katrina."

61

"I am." She pulled the wrinkles from her starched white lab jacket and pushed out her ample chest as far as decency allowed. There was her red-yellow-green Wellington Labs official nametag: Katrina Raider. Bold and black, clearly readable.

Rigger's jaw had already dropped. There was nothing left to drop. He could only stare at this stranger with the other woman's name sewn to her left breast and wonder what happened.

Ms. Raider waited a long time for Rigger's expression to change; it didn't. When no explanation of his obvious shock at seeing her was evident, she spoke.

"You seem to know me."

Rigger apologized once more. "It's just...I thought you–that is, Katrina, Miss Raider–was younger."

"Well," she said. "I'm not that old." Her expression clouded, growing decidedly colder.

"No, no. I didn't mean it that way." Rigger tried to think fast. "If I wasn't a happily married man, I'd ask you out to dinner. You look to be about my age."

Her eyes softened. She fluffed up her beehive hairdo and batted her Mabellines.

"I didn't mean to startle you." He regained some semblance of composure. "It's my first time working this building, and my niece, another Katrina Raider, works in a laboratory like this one." He swept his hand around, to help construct his lie. "Her mother told me about it. When I saw her name–that is, your name–on the door, I assumed I'd stumbled onto the place where she works. She's about twenty-two. That's why I made the inane remark about your age."

"I see."

Realizing she was somewhat mollified, Rigger decided he'd better beat a retreat before she began asking questions he couldn't answer. He took up her trashcan, dumped it into his rollaway barrel, and with a cheery, "Goodnight," he went for the door.

"Hey," Miss Raider said. "Wait a minute."

Rigger stopped, his heart pounding.

"You forgot one." She pointed to another trash container, under the table.

"Oh," Rigger said, "so I did."

By the time he dumped that one into his wheeled drum, the dedicated Katrina Raider was back at work on her glass slides, studying a zoo of microscopic gremlins.

* * * * *

"Just when I thought I had her all figured out," Rigger said to Pugsley over lunch at Hannibal's Café the next day, "I run into another Katrina Raider." He took a bite of fried liver and chewed for a minute. "What do you make of all this, Pug? Two Katrina Raiders in the same city?"

"She leaves tracks like an alcoholic rattlesnake. I thought I had her cold."

"So did I. Especially after I got a peek at Rachel's stomach when she tumbled with Wolf on the floor and saw that hideous scar. The poor kid. She's been through so much misery, yet she takes all that life hands her and skips along, seemingly unconcerned. Did I tell you how that kid can play make-believe? She can become a ballerina, a puppy, or even a fish, just like..." Rigger began a gesture that would have ended with his fingers snapping in the air, but his friend's expression stopped him in mid-motion.

Pugsley's eyes were wide, a bite of black-eyed peas halfway to his open mouth. "That's it!" He dropped his fork, needing his hands to talk.

"That's what?" Rigger didn't get both words out before Pugsley spilled his thoughts.

"That sneaky snake. She assumed someone else's name."

"Well, of course she did. She took Katrina Raider's name."

"You should have asked that real Katrina what her address is. I'll lay you odds it's twenty-three-oh-one Kimberley Lane, Number twenty-one. Your little dove didn't take her name, she took the whole works—address, car, degree in that ethnobotany stuff, everything."

"Why?" Rigger asked.

"It's a scam."

Rigger wrinkled his brow.

"She—and I'll bet there's an accomplice hiding in the bushes, probably a man—is scamming you for something."

"What?"

"What do you have, other than money?"

"That's all. Just money."

"What about that secret government project you never talk about?"

"A spy?" Rigger whispered.

Pugsley leaned back in the padded booth, folding his arms across his chest, and fixed Rigger with his smile. "Either that or your money."

Chapter Eight

Rigger read through the report again, the one Pugsley filched from Sgt. Robolinski's computer about the murder of Rachel's parents—the man wearing the rubber mask, dancing around his young woman accomplice as she butchered the victims. And the most chilling of all—the "sharp wire thingie" around the woman's neck, as the little girl described it to the police.

"A barbed wire choker tattoo," Rigger whispered. He dropped the page to the table. "The same freaks. The same ones who killed my wife and daughter."

This was just the sort of coincidence poets love and engineers hate. A poet would see the irony, the hidden messages, and the beauty of it all coming together in some cosmic reality. An engineer, skeptical until each and every factoid had been rolled onto its backside and thoroughly examined, would never believe his exposure to two events so similar in detail to be mere happenstance.

Something else is afoot here.

He leaned back in his chair and laced his fingers behind his head. Rigger was no poet.

After a moment, he picked up the report and flipped the pages, looking for something.

"When that lady came to save me," Rigger read

Rachel's words from the report, "she shot her gun, and that mask fell off the man. Big, ugly face. They ran away with a car. Then the nice lady grabbed me and held tight. She cried, too."

* * * * *

Monday dawned, grimy and cold, then faded into a sunless chain-gray forenoon. Rigger built a fire in the fireplace to brighten up the place.

An hour later, he put down the book he'd been reading, *How to Manage Women*, by Norman Bates, and went to the door. He knew it was Katrina and Rachel—they came by almost every day now, around mid-afternoon. Wolf also knew who it was. He ran ahead of Rigger and waited eagerly for the door to open.

While Katrina busied herself around the apartment, Rigger sat on the edge of his chair and strummed an old guitar, adjusting the B string. Henry the Barbie doll sat beside him, waiting. She always waited in happy anticipation for something, anything, to happen.

Rachel played with Wolf nearby. They tugged on opposite ends of a twisted piece of cowhide, the kind they sell at pet stores for one's dog to gnaw at, rather than the furniture. Wolf growled from the sides of his mouth, and Rachel giggled as she tried to wrest it from his jaws.

Rigger began to sing "Scarborough Fair." His voice was a mellow baritone, and he sang with a crisp Irish accent.

Rachel stopped when she heard the music. She let go of the piece of hide, and the puppy tumbled over backward. When he jumped to his feet, he dropped the hide of contention and watched the girl with a perplexed look on his face. She wandered over in front of Rigger,

66

settling down at his feet. With her elbow on a knee, she cupped her chin and watched him in awed reverence.

Rigger winked at her and began the second verse. When he finished the song, Rachel shouted, "Again," and clapped her hands. She then added in a softer tone, "Please," drawing out the last "e" and giving him her cutest little girl tilt of head and a crinkly-eyed smile.

He played and sang for her, and she joined him on the refrain, mimicking his tone, inflection, and accent.

By the fourth time through, Rachel knew it all, every word by heart. He played the song once more but kept silent, letting her sing by herself. Her dolce contralto sounded like warm honey pouring onto a just-from-the-oven muffin—sweet and velvety smooth. It was then he heard a quiet footfall and saw Katrina walking, head bowed, back to the kitchen, wiping something from her cheek with a tea towel.

When Rigger began a lively Irish jig, Rachel leapt to her feet and began to dance. There was no recognizable pattern to her dancing; her feet just moved to the music.

Wolf became excited by the sounds and girl's dancing. He barked and jumped at her feet. Rachel stepped on the dog's leg and tried to get off the yelping puppy without hurting him. She lost her balance and threw out her hands to break her fall.

Rigger was on his feet as soon as she tripped, tossing aside the guitar. But he couldn't get to her in time. She hit the edge of the oak coffee table and screamed in pain.

He scooped her up and ran for the kitchen. Katrina ran toward them.

"What happened?" she shouted.

"She fell and hit the edge of the table."

Rachel yelled and squirmed around, trying to get

out of his arms. Blood poured from her mouth.

"Let me see, baby." Katrina tried to pull the girl's hands from her mouth.

"Mommy, Mommy!" she cried and fought away Katrina's hands.

"I'm right here, sweetheart. Let me see your lip."

"NO!" she cried. "I want my real mommy."

Katrina glanced up at Rigger and tried again to get Rachel's hands away so she could see the damage.

Finally, Rigger was able to hold Rachel's hands so Katrina could examine the girl's mouth. She carefully lifted her already swelling upper lip and wiggled the girl's front teeth. Rachel bit down on her fingers. Katrina jerked back her hand and shook it to relieve the pain.

"Her teeth are definitely okay."

The blood covering Katrina's hand soaked Rachel's collar and the front of her little blouse.

"Check the inside of her lip," Rigger snapped.

When Katrina gently lifted the lip, they saw the ugly gash where the blood poured out.

"Do you think she needs stitches?" Katrina asked.

"No. Get some ice." He then cooed to Rachel, "It's going to be okay, sweetheart. I'll take care of you. Don't worry, everything's going to be fine."

He let go of her hands, and she hit him, then scratched his face, still twisting around in his arms, trying to get away from the pain. Once more, she cried for her mother.

Katrina brought an ice cube and held it against Rachel's lip. The child cried and tried to push away Katrina. After a few minutes, she calmed down, and the flow of blood slowed.

Rigger eased himself down on the love seat, holding her close. Katrina sat beside him and made a motion, offering to take her, but Rigger shook his head.

An hour later, he still held her. She was asleep, having cried herself to exhaustion. Blood soaked his new blue shirt. The bleeding had finally stopped. Her lip was swollen out of proportion, but the cut wasn't deep enough to require medical attention. She would be okay.

"Why did she yell for her mother," Rigger asked, "when you were right there?"

"I-I don't know," Katrina stammered. "I guess she was just hysterical with the pain and didn't recognize me." She glanced from the girl's face to him. "She tried to fight you off, too." She smiled and reached out to touch the four little scratches on his face.

"Yeah." He looked down at the beautiful sleeping face of the little angel in his arms.

"You better let me have that shirt," she said. "I'll wash it for you before the stain sets."

When he looked up at her, the smile was still on her lips.

* * * * *

Rigger changed his shirt after laying Rachel down on the love seat, then went to the drugstore for some liquid baby aspirin. When he returned to the apartment thirty minutes later, he was met by the unmistakable smell of spaghetti sauce cooking in the kitchen. He also heard the sound of the washing machine going into a spin cycle.

Rachel sat on the love seat, her head lying on the arm. Henry sat in the same position, her head on Rachel's thigh. Rachel didn't raise her head; only gave him a little wave. She reached to Henry without looking, and Henry gave Rigger a little wave also.

"Where's Mama?" he asked.

"Doing lookstick."

"Lookstick?"

Rachel made a motion across her lower lip with her fingertip.

"Ah, lipstick." He looked toward the kitchen, then sat beside Rachel on the love seat. He opened the carton containing the baby aspirin. "I want you to take some of this, sweetheart. It'll make you feel better." She wore a little nightgown, and Rigger wondered where it came from. He had nothing like that in his apartment.

She lifted her head and looked up at him, at the side of his face.

"I sorry, God," she whispered.

He smiled and held the plastic dropper to her lips. She sucked the medicine into her mouth as he squeezed the bulb.

"It's nothing," he said. "Didn't hurt a bit."

He put away the aspirin and picked her up. She slipped her arms around his neck, and he held her tight for a minute. He then took her to his chair, put her down, and switched on the TV. He flipped the channels, looking for a cartoon show.

"I want you to sit still and take it easy. That medicine'll start to work in a minute, and you'll feel much better."

She nodded and watched the SpongeBob show.

Rigger laid the remote controller on the arm of the chair, brushed her wet hair from her forehead, and kissed her. She smiled up at him and snuggled back in his chair. After he got Henry and handed the doll to Rachel, she cradled it in her arm.

Wolf whined at his feet. Rigger snapped his fingers and pointed at the empty place beside Rachel in the chair. The puppy jumped to the chair, turned around two times, then settled down with his head on his paws and watched the TV. Rigger went to the kitchen.

"What is that delightful smell?" he asked.

"I just thought I'd fix us—I mean you, a little dinner before we leave."

"Great. What can I do?"

She sliced a tomato into quarters. "Can you make a salad?"

Rigger glanced at her strawberry-red lips. *Nice lookstick.*

"Ha. Can I?" He washed his hands and went to the refrigerator to get the lettuce.

He stood at the open refrigerator door, looking her over as she stirred the sauce with a wooden spoon. He let his eyes roam the length of her body, head to heels, and back up. He then noticed something and cocked his head: she had a wallet in the hip pocket of her tight blue jeans. Apparently, she always carried it, because the outline was worn into the fabric.

Strange. She had a purse when she came in. Why not carry the wallet in her purse? It's not her phone; that's in the other hip pocket.

Rigger saw her glance at her watch. He checked the digital display on the microwave; it was almost 5:30 p.m.

He closed the refrigerator, forgetting about the salad. "When do you have to be at the lab?"

She stopped stirring and whipped her head around toward him.

Rigger smiled.

She stared out the kitchen window for a moment, studying the bare-limbed elms planted on the roof of the building next door. The branches swayed in the gathering darkness.

"How much do you know?"

"I know the real Katrina Raider has to report to work at Wellington Labs by six o'clock. And I know she's over fifty years old."

She dropped the spoon on the countertop, wiped her hands on a towel, and faced him. "You've been spying on me."

He took a step toward her.

She flipped the towel over her shoulder but didn't back away. "Why?" she whispered, staring up at him.

"Because I thought you were a spy. When you—" The doorbell rang, loud and irritating. "Who the heck could that be?" He hurried to the front door as the bell rang again.

"Wow, Rig." Pugsley stood in Rigger's doorway, taking a deep breath. "You're cooking something different tonight."

"Hey, Pug. What's up?"

"Oh, sorry." Pugsley looked at Rachel and her Barbie doll sitting in front of the TV. He then whispered, "Didn't know you had company. I just wanted to see how you're doing."

"Hello, there." Katrina came toward them from the kitchen. "Friend of yours?" she asked Rigger.

"Uh...sometimes."

"I'm Katrina Raider." She extended her hand to Pugsley.

"Theodore Olympus Breckinridge." He took her hand and put on the softest expression Rigger had ever seen.

For a moment, he imagined Pugsley was going to fold himself at the waist and kiss her hand. "Olympus?" Rigger asked. He couldn't keep from grinning at his pal.

"We'll talk about that later." Pugsley let go of Katrina's hand. "Call me Pugsley, or Pug."

"Okay, Pug." She smiled. "That fits you better

anyway. Most people call me Cat."

"Ah," Pugsley said, "a cat burglar, huh?"

"Well, only as a hobby." No one laughed. "Joke," she said, glancing at Rigger. "I can make a joke, can't I? You made a joke about the maid you don't have."

"Ha," Rigger forced a laugh.

Pugsley looked from one to the other. "Rig, you remember 'Leven-finger Louie? Now, there was a cat burglar. Could crawl right up the granite side of a bank building in the rain, he could."

"'Leven-finger Louie?" Katrina said, with a laugh. "Did he really have eleven fingers?"

"Yep," Pugsley said, holding up his right hand and spreading the fingers. "An extra pinky right here between these two middle ones."

"Get out!" Katrina punched him on the shoulder.

Rigger wondered if this was the real Katrina. Could she be feigning sweetness and laughter as part of her act? She'd certainly fooled him with an expert job of being a streetwise shrew. Both he and Pugsley knew she was a fraud, trying to worm her way into his confidence for some reason. Probably, like Pugsley said, having designs on being his beneficiary.

If that's the case, why isn't she sweet and kind to me? And just how nice is she going to be to Pugsley?

"See you later, pal," Rigger threatened to close the door on his friend, who still stood on the threshold.

"Rigger!" Katrina said. "Pug looks hungry. Have you had dinner?"

"Nope."

"He's not hungry, and he has urgent business somewhere." Rigger fixed his stare on Pugsley and gave him an exaggerated wink.

"It can wait." Either Pugsley missed the signal, or

he ignored it. He sniffed the air. "Sage…" He took another breath. "Cayenne pepper, and…" he wrinkled his brow, "sweet basil?"

"Yep," she said, "and a smidgen of nutmeg."

"Nutmeg! Yes, the prefect touch."

Katrina and Pugsley grinned like twin Cheshire cats balled up in some sort of scheme to sidetrack Rigger.

"Come in, Pug," Rigger said, with resignation. "Before the two of you OD on seasonings and I have to clean up the mess." He waved him in and closed the door.

"Is that a whiff of French bread I detect in the air?" Pugsley asked.

"Yes, and the first loaf is about ready to come out of the oven. Come give me a hand. I've got to start on the gingerbread muffins." Over her shoulder, she then said, "Rigger, would you check on Rachel for me?"

"I'd be happy to," he said to their backs.

Seldom in his life had Rigger relegated responsibilities to anyone. He was always in control of his actions. But now, in the twilight of his total defeat, he wanted someone else to make decisions for him. It was more difficult every day to separate similar courses of action. Harder to decide between simple things, like turning left or right at an intersection when his destination had been forgotten or tangled up with some other duty clambering for his attention.

Not only was his life confusing him, he'd foolishly taken up with a woman and little girl. Somewhere in the deep recesses of his rotting brain, the two of them were trying to replace his lost wife and daughter. Was that Katrina's purpose? Knowing everything about him, was she planning ahead to the time when he'd become a bedridden invalid and she'd be the only person close enough to him to take over his affairs, including his assets? In that case, why did she instantly take up with Pugsley, his closest friend?

Too complicated, he decided. But one thing he was sure of: he was jealous.

He found the girl sitting quietly in his chair. "Can I play some music for you, Miss Rachel?"

Her face brightened, and she rewarded him with a smile.

While delicious aromas of Katrina and Pugsley's revelry in exotic seasonings wafted from the kitchen and filled the apartment with titillating promises of a tasty dinner, he strummed the guitar and thought about what he could play for his little girl.

He played "Ghost Riders in the Sky," then "Band of Gold."

"Would you like to hear about a lost city?"

Her eyes widened, and she nodded.

After a few chords, he began to sing.

> *I was on my wa-ay to Valdacia-a,*
> *far across the deep blue sea-a,*
> *I'd searched so long, it seems,*
> *for that great lost city of dreams.*
>
> *Along the trail one sunny day-a,*
> *I met three friends going my way-a,*
> *I bowed low to the leader,*
> *and said howdy to her.*

"Dinner's ready," Katrina called from the other room.

Rigger put aside the guitar and picked up Rachel to take her to the dining room.

When Rigger, Rachel, and Katrina were seated, Rigger glanced at Rachel. She had a forlorn look. The food smelled delicious. There was spaghetti with meat sauce, salad with Thousand Island dressing, and French bread. But it was obvious with her cut and swollen lip, she'd never be able to eat any of it.

Katrina caught Rigger's eye and winked at him. She tapped her glass with a spoon and said toward the kitchen, "Waiter, please bring that special tray for our very special guest."

Pugsley came in, singing, *"I was on my way to Valdacia-a."* He carried a silver tray and placed it in front of Rachel as Katrina whisked away the girl's plate.

Rachel beamed. On her tray was a cup of chocolate milk, with little marshmallows and a straw to help her get the sweet liquid past her cut lip. There was also a gingerbread muffin, just from the oven, cut in little pieces, with butter melting into it.

Everyone waited while she placed the straw in the drink and took a sip through the corner of her mouth. She smiled up at Pugsley and gave him a thumb and finger circle.

"I love brown milk," she said. "How did you know that?"

"Oh," Pugsley said as he went to his seat on the opposite side of the table. "A little puppy told me."

"For goodness cakes," Rachel said.

"Where did you two meet?" Katrina asked as she passed Pugsley the salad bowl.

"In the circus." Pugsley took the bowl and dug into the salad.

"Circus?" Katrina and Rachel cried together.

"Oh, no." Rigger groaned. He pressed his hands to his face. "Pug," he whispered as he wearily slipped his hands down his face, "you're not going to tell that story. They don't want to hear all that old garbage."

"Yes, we do." Katrina said. "Did you say at the circus, or in the circus?"

"In."

"Oh, we're definitely going to hear all about this." She smiled at Rigger, who was obviously in wretched discomfort.

"What did he do in the circus?" Rachel asked. "Was he a cannonball man?"

"Nope." Pugsley chewed a bite of salad.

"But he was a performer, wasn't he?" Katrina sipped her iced tea and eyed Rigger, who looked at her and shook his head, hoping she wouldn't pursue much more.

"Well, I guess so. He was the lion tamer."

Before Katrina or Rachel could respond with more questions, Rigger said, "That's nothing. Tell them what you were, Pug."

"What?" Rachel asked, her eyes wide with excitement.

"He was a clown," Rigger said.

"Get outta town!" Katrina cried. "Rachel, we're having dinner with a clown and a lion tamer!"

"Yea!" Rachel squealed and clapped her hands over her head. "A clown!" She looked upon Pugsley with as much admiration as she could possibly load onto him.

Pugsley did some magic tricks with silverware and napkins. The ladies clapped their hands, while Rigger smiled and watched the others enjoy themselves. He couldn't understand the slight twinge of guilt he felt.

I can't be gloomy all the time. Especially when everyone is having such a good time.

Yes, he had to admit it, the company was delightful, and the sound of happy voices lifted his spirits higher than they'd been in months. Nothing wrong with that.

"Do your juggling thing," he said to Pug.

Pugsley jumped to his feet. "Okay, but you gotta help me. Man, I should'a wore my pink polka-dot jacket with the big pockets. Oh well, I can fake it...I think."

Rigger stood, and as soon as Pugsley nodded to him, he picked up a muffin and tossed it to Pugsley, who caught it and began arching it in the air. Rigger tossed him a whole tomato Katrina had placed on the table for decoration. Pugsley caught that and juggled it with the muffin. Rigger threw him the bread knife, very sharp. Rachel and Katrina oohed and ahed. Rigger then beat a drum roll on the table with his fingers as the ladies watched and waited. Rigger tossed him a burning candle. Pugsley deftly caught it and juggled it with the knife, muffin, and tomato.

The candle was one of those that re-lights itself when someone tries to blow it out. The flame kept going out, leaving a smoky trail in the air, then it would reignite when Pug caught it.

Katrina and Rachel clapped and cheered for him.

Another drum roll from Rigger, longer and louder. Suddenly, Pugsley grabbed the knife from the air, sliced the tomato in two, impaled the two halves on his knife blade, topped off by the gingerbread muffin, then, with a loud "Ta-Daaaa" from Rigger, caught the smoking candle between his teeth, at which point the flame came back to life.

Katrina and Rachel jumped to their feet, clapping and yelling for Pugsley. Rigger clapped and whistled. Pugsley threw the burning candle to Rigger and bowed deeply to the ladies.

"Thank you, one and all," he said, with a smile. "Too bad the snakes aren't here." He gestured toward Rigger. "My old circus buddy could make them jump through hoops."

"Well," Rigger said as he placed the candle back into the holder. "Cocker spaniels and Dalmatians, maybe, but snakes? I could never get them to jump very high."

* * * * *

At half past ten, Pugsley said he had to be going. Rachel had fallen asleep in his lap, and Katrina took her as Pugsley got to his feet.

"Pug's a great guy," Katrina said after Pugsley left.

"Yeah, best friend I ever had."

"You were really in the circus?"

"Well, not an actual traveling circus. It was just a charity event at Rockefeller Center. There were lots of volunteers, and he and I were just two of hundreds."

"Can I ask a favor?" she said.

"Sure."

"Do you mind if Rachel and I spend the night?"

Now this was a surprise. That was the last thing Rigger expected, and she was almost nice about it.

"Well..." He wasn't sure how to respond. Of course it was all right; he just wondered about the sleeping arrangements.

"We could use one of the upstairs bedrooms. We're as quiet as two little mice. You'll never know we're here."

"Sure, that's fine. By the way, I've been wondering where her nightgown came from."

"I always keep one in my bag. We never know where...I mean, we never know when she might need it. I've got one for me, too." Katrina paused, smiling up at him. "You wanna see it?"

79

Chapter Nine

Wolf woke Rigger early the next morning, ready to go outside. The puppy was finally housebroken, and Rigger didn't want the dog to backslide into his old habit of making little puddles on the floor. He dressed quietly and went to the kitchen, with Wolf at his heels. He started a pot of coffee, enough for two. It would be ready when they came back in, then maybe he and Katrina could have a little talk.

The sun wasn't up yet, but the dark clouds showed patches of gray. Snow continued to fall, and more than twelve inches had accumulated. The wind had died, leaving huge drifts at every lamppost and trashcan.

"Must have snowed all night," Rigger whispered to the dog as he closed the front door of the apartment building behind him.

The puppy leapt into the snow just as he did everything—with zeal and excitement. He found a small drift at the base of the steps and disappeared beneath the snow. He immediately porpoised up above the snow, then went under again, then once more until he was on the sidewalk, where the wind had swept the snow down to a few inches. He plowed along, glancing back at Rigger. His eyes were bright, and his little tongue hung out the side of his mouth. The puppy's fuzzy tail swished as he broke trail for his master.

Rigger saw two sets of footprints that came down the steps and turned left. They were only dim impressions now, almost filled with new snow. He didn't think much of them; just two people leaving his apartment building earlier in the morning.

Wolf went to the right, as he always did, and Rigger followed. The snow was completely virgin in that direction, no footprints at all. The streetlights were still on, and the snow fell softly through cones of greenish light. There was no traffic or pedestrians anywhere. Snow covered the dirt and trash and hung in thick layers on the shrubs and trees along the street. A truly beautiful sight, lovely and refreshing. And it was deathly silent.

The soft, white landscape with gentle, flowing curves over lawns and hedges lying quietly in the defused light of dawn made him think of Katrina. "Cat," she'd told Pugsley. She didn't extend the same courtesy to Rigger, but he wondered how she'd react if he called her "Cat." He imagined her, back at his apartment. She and Rachel curled up together in his bed, sleeping peacefully...well, not really his bed, but a bed in one of the rooms upstairs. He didn't even know which bedroom they were in.

She did give him a glimpse of her long blue nightgown when she pulled it from her bag and held it up by the thin spaghetti straps.

"Mamma!" Rachel had startled both of them. "Don't let him see your nightie."

They both thought the girl was asleep as she nestled in comfortable recliner.

Katrina stuffed the flimsy silk gown back into her purse.

"I didn't see a thing, sweetheart," Rigger said as he kissed the girl on the cheek. "I only saw your pretty face."

Rachel gave him a hug, then he watched the two of them go upstairs to bed.

Wolf went right at the corner, knowing exactly where to go. Rigger didn't care; he was just happy to be out in the frigid air, in the refreshing new world of white. He did, however, have that uneasy feeling again. The first time it came to him was two days before, when he walked home from the daycare center, as if someone watched him.

The puppy stopped under a bush and lifted his leg. Rigger glanced back the way they'd come, but no one was there. No movement anywhere. He shook off the feeling as Wolf pulled him on down the street. Now they were on the street behind his apartment, and soon they'd go back up to his street.

When they got to the corner of his street, Rigger tugged on the leash to stop the dog for a moment. He listened but heard nothing.

"Let's go home, Wolf."

Ahead of him, in the virgin snow, were a set of fresh footprints leaving a doorway and walking the same way he and Wolf had gone when they first came outside. He knew for sure those footprints hadn't been there earlier, and the doorway they came out of was a flower shop that didn't open until nine. As Rigger walked, he placed his boot next to one of the footprints. It was almost two inches larger than his.

"Pretty big guy," he whispered.

The tracks passed his apartment house doorway and followed Rigger and Wolf's footprints they'd made just a few minutes before.

What a jerk. He's smart enough to stay out of sight, but too dumb to realize he's leaving tracks in the snow. Rigger looked back. *He must be right around the corner behind us.*

After Rigger stepped inside the building and closed the door, he stood with his back to the wall, watching the sidewalk through the glass door. After waiting five minutes, no one walked by, so he and Wolf went to the elevator.

When they got inside his apartment, he locked the door, and after Wolf shook himself, Rigger unlatched the leash from the collar so the puppy could run to check on Rachel. But he didn't go to the stairs leading to the spare bedrooms. Instead, he ran to the kitchen.

Well, Rigger thought, with a smile, *they must be up already.*

He shook the snow from his overcoat in the foyer and hung it on one of the pegs of the coat track. In the kitchen, he found Wolf munching his dog food. No one else was there.

When Rigger went upstairs and knocked at the first bedroom door, there was no answer. He quietly opened the door to see the bed made up and the room looking as if it hadn't been used. There was no response at the second bedroom either. When he opened that door, he saw the bed was made, but when he walked in, he was sure the room had been occupied. He didn't know how he could tell, but something about the room told him someone had spent the night there.

He saw a note on the pillow. His stomach churned into a cramp. He opened the folded page of baby-blue paper, knowing it was bad news.

Before he began to read, he realized what it was about the room that made it feel lived in—perfume. He hadn't noticed it the night before, but now he knew she'd worn perfume the previous evening. It wasn't an overpowering scent; more of a hint of lilacs on a spring morning. That's what made the room alive, her perfume.

"Hi, Rig," he read. "We had to leave early and didn't want to wake you. I hope you don't mind, we had some milk and gingerbread before we left. Rachel and Henry said bye and luv." She signed it, "Cat," followed by a smiley face with long cat whiskers and two more smaller ones without whiskers.

"Cat," he whispered. He pulled down the bedspread and picked up one of the pillows, pressing it gently to his face.

Chapter Ten

In the air, over Anddor Shallau

Sasha and Nikita flew their Sukhoi SU-57 fighters at 5,000 meters over the Safandel desert, in central Anddor Shallau.

A block of static came from Sasha's earpiece, followed by her wingman's words. "*Mogu li ya prisest' zdes* (We have visitors),"Nikita said.

Sasha touched the 360-degree display button on her stick. "*Izvinite* (Where)?"she asked.

"*U menya vsyo normal'no* (Ten o'clock low)."

Sasha tilted her head to her left and looked toward the ten o'clock low position.

Sensors inside her helmet picked up her head and eye motion, then displayed the lower left quadrant on the inside of her visor.

"*Do svidaniya* (I see them)." She zoomed her display. "*Mogu li ya priset' zdes* (My radar did not pick them up)."

"*Gde nakhoditsya tualet* (They are just as stealthy as we are)."

"F-35C," Sasha said.

Two blocks of static came back, confirming Sasha's identification of the other fighters. "F-35 affirmative. Are they Israeli?"

"No, not the 'C' variation."

"How can you know they are 'C'?" Nikita asked.

"Tail hook. These bandits came off a carrier."

"Carrier? Persian Gulf?"

"Probably."

"Must be American, and they are a long way from home," Nikita said.

"Their range is approx twenty-two hundred kilometers."

"The gulf is over nine hundred clicks south of here."

"Uh-huh." She watched the F35s fly under her at 500 meters altitude, then they started a slow rotation to the west.

"If they came off a carrier in the Gulf," Nikita said, "they have to be low on fuel."

"Let us find out." She checked Nikita's position— twenty meters off her right tail fin. "Come up on my right wing, and stay there."

"Copy."

Sasha rolled over onto her left wing, banking down and to the south.

Nikita stayed with her like a silver shadow.

Sasha watched the F35s on her visor display as they preformed an identical maneuver.

She smiled, then rolled to her back and dove toward the desert below.

The F35s duplicated her movements.

Sasha hit her afterburners. "Now, let us burn some of their precious fuel."

Two blocks of static came from her earpiece.

She pulled out of her dive at 100 meters, scaring the

hell out of three camels and stirring up a cloud of dust. She climbed her SU-57 straight up at 2400 kilometers-per-hour—almost three times the speed of sound.

Looking out the right side of her canopy, she saw Nikita give her an agitated hand signal, pointing to her left. She looked that way and gasped into her oxygen mask; the two F35s were flying in formation with her, just ten meters off her wingtip.

The pilot in the closest aircraft touched two fingers to his visor.

She smiled, gave him a salute, then pointed toward the sky.

He nodded and throttled up.

Sasha did the same.

As they climbed, he tapped his helmet, over his right ear. He held up two fingers, then five fingers, then two again.

She switched to frequency 252 on her radio. "Hello, Hotshot."

"Good morning, Red One." He pointed to the nose art on her aircraft. "What does that rabbit have between his legs?"

"We call that a missile."

They stayed side-by-side for thirty seconds. The closest F35 had a tiger with flaming wings painted on the fuselage, beside the cockpit.

She checked her fuel gauge; the needle sank past the one-half mark and drifted downward.

Ten seconds later, the F35s peeled off, heading south.

Sasha and Nikita leveled off at 8,000 meters. She spoke into her mic. "Goodbye, Yankee tiger."

Static came back, then, "See you later, alligator."

"That is Miss Alligator. You run now back to carrier

Reagan in Persian waters. Think you gas tanks come dry little bit.”

“Hey, how the fu—I mean, we go now back fine Japanese airplane place, thank you very much.”

She laughed. “Then maybe you fly wrong way for Tokyo, tiger bull liar.”

“Ha ha ha. See you at the Red October in Moscow Saturday night. You can buy me a Molotov cocktail.”

“What you talking Moscow? I been come straight outta Jersey.” She noticed her wingman tapping the left side of his helmet, near his ear.

She changed her radio frequency back to 5617.0.

“...on the road from Zebec,” came over her earpiece.

“Control,” she said, “repeat.”

“Primary target is on the road from Zebec.”

“Copy. Coordinates?”

“One-sixteen by three thirty-seven.”

“One-sixteen by three thirty-seven,” she said. “We’re on our way.”

“We count twenty-three long-bed transports and four troop carriers.”

“Jackpot!” She tapped her navigation button, bringing up the coordinate position on her display. Then to her wingman, she said, “Let us go hunting, Nikita.”

“Copy that.”

* * * * *

“Good morning, Bunny Babuska.” Rio flew his F-35 up beside Sasha’s plane.

“Ha ha. Hello, Grandpa Tiger.”

“I prefer ‘Rio.’”

“Okay, Rio. I am Sasha.”

“Glad to meet you.” He scanned the horizon around

the Safandel desert. "Where's your wingman?"

This was the day after their first encounter.

"He go to wedding today."

"Ah, good for him."

"It is his wedding," she said.

"Ah, too bad." He did a barrel roll over the top of her, coming out ten meters off her right wingtip.

"I see they let you come out to play by yourself." She peeled off to the left.

He followed, flying beneath her. "They think I'm over Afghanistan."

"I pretty sure they know exactly where you're flying." She pulled straight up into a vertical loop.

Rio dropped back behind her, watching the glow of her afterburner.

"I see you checking out my tailpipes."

He laughed. "Just trying to light my cigar."

"Watch this." She flipped over, applied full flaps, and killed her engines.

He shot past her at 1900 kph. "Cool move."

Sasha reignited her engines and caught up with him, flying upside down, just off his left wing.

For five minutes, they did an erotic dance in the sky. There was no communications; just long, smooth, matching aerial maneuvers, like a waltz between two thirty-five-million-dollar dancers burning five hundred dollars' worth of fuel a minute.

"See those thunderhead over there?" Rio asked.

She looked where he pointed. "Un-huh."

"Check this out." He hit his afterburners and accelerated toward the biggest of the towering cumulus monsters.

"I do not think that is such a good idea, Rio."

"You fly like a girl." He disappeared into the boiling

thunderhead.

Ten seconds passed. "Rio?"

He blasted out of the cloud, a half-kilometer above her. "Wow, that was scary."

"You are one crazy son-of-a-bitc—"

"Missile!" Rio yelled. "On your six, low. Break right!" He peeled off in the opposite direction.

Sasha jerked her stick to the right and released a dozen decoy flares.

The missile zeroed in on the hottest flare as Sasha escaped toward the ground.

"Whew, that was close, Rio. Did your pal do that?"

"No, it came from the ground. Probably your Fidai Mahaz comrades, trying to hit me."

"Well, maybe you should go over—"

"Shit! Sasha! Another one. Five hundred meters, coming at your butt!"

Sasha pulled up, but too late. The missile exploded on her left vertical stabilizer, destroying the whole tail section and sending debris flying along the hull, ripping into the wings and fuselage. Her aircraft spiraled into a dive as she struggled for control.

A secondary explosion in her left engine sent a broken titanium strut slicing through the back of the cockpit and into her right leg.

She screamed and tried to push away the serrated strut as she fought for control of the diving aircraft.

"Get out!" Rio yelled. "Bail out of there!"

"Eject not working. Shit! Trying manual."

"Damn it! Can you pop the canopy?"

A second later, the canopy blew away.

Rio flew down toward her.

"Fucking leg trapped. Can not—"

He heard her breath coming hard and ragged.

"Bail!" he yelled. "Bail now! You're headed for the ground!"

"Trying to cut this damn—"

Seconds ticked away. "Sasha! Get out now!"

Suddenly, her ejection seat blasted free of the aircraft. She popped her straps loose, falling away from the tumbling seat. Her chute opened just before her plane exploded on a hillside below, sending up a greasy cloud of smoke and fire. Her red and white striped chute billowed out as she drifted through the smoke.

"Wow," Rio whispered. "She made it." He circled around, watching her float toward a line of sand dunes.

A few seconds later, he saw her hit the sand fifty meters from the burning plane. She released her chute, stood, and yanked off her helmet, releasing a flood of flaming red hair.

He swooped low to see her struggle to stand. As he flew by, she gave him a thumbs-up.

Okay. Now I just have to get her some help.

He switched to the Russian Air Force frequency. "Mayday, mayday. Your SU-57 shot down by surface to air missile. Northern Anddor Shallau."

"Who is talking? Get off military frequency."

"This is Captain Rio Lujan, U.S. Air Force. Flying recon over Safandel desert. Saw SU-57 hit by a missile. Maybe one of your S-400. The pilot got out. She's on the ground."

"Ha, yes, and I am probably President Trump riding donkey down to Weisconsen."

"Listen, her plane had a bunny rabbit riding a missile, painted on the nose. She's on the ground, and she needs help. Now!"

"Ah, stand by one."

Rio clicked his mic button twice.

"Okay. See Sasha missing on radar. Give location."

He flew over her and clicked his GPS locator. "51.91 North, 69.41 East."

"Copy 51.91 North, 69.41 East."

Two clicks.

"We send helicopters from Kimglard."

Two clicks.

Rio looked toward the northern horizon. *Kimglard, one hundred kilometers away. Over an hour before their choppers get here.*

He circled, flew toward her at five hundred meters altitude, waggling his wings.

She waved to him, then started climbing the sand dune, but her right leg collapsed, and she fell, tumbling down the dune.

Shit. She's injured.

He checked his fuel level.

Can't hang around much longer.

He flew to a thousand meters altitude.

Let's see if there's any friendlies around here.

He made a wide circle, checking for villages.

Nothing. One more circuit, then I've got to head for the carrier.

A few minutes later, he spotted a plume of dust rising on the wind. He turned toward it and saw two vehicles, driving fast along a dry ravine.

I thought they were sending choppers. Better go down and take a look.

He flew past them, low to the deck and a hundred meters away.

Machine guns on top of both the troop carriers opened up on him.

"Holy shit! Maha ja dein! And they're heading right for her." Rio knew the Russian jets had been strafing the Maha ja dein truck convoys going into the Safandel region.

They wouldn't treat a Russian fighter pilot kindly.

He pulled up to a thousand meters and headed north. The column of black smoke from the crash site was less than a kilometer from the two racing trucks. He lined up on the trucks and flew over Sasha at two hundred meters altitude, then targeted the lead truck.

He fired a sidewinder missile into the radiator of the first vehicle, then veered away to the right as the truck exploded. The second truck careened off the road, then jockeyed back onto the dirt track, ahead of the burning truck. It accelerated toward Sasha's crash site.

Rio came around from the rear of the truck and fired his second sidewinder into its tailgate, blowing the vehicle to bits.

He flew over Sasha, waggled his wings, and turned south, heading for home.

That's all I can do for you, kid. He glanced at his fuel gauge. *I'll be running on fumes by the time I get to the Persian Gulf.*

* * * * *

"*Sazhalyeneeyoo mnye para Brezhnev eettee* (You are still off flight status, Major Brezhnev)."

Sasha dropped into a chair and rubbed her stiff right leg. "*Vi gavareetye paTU-95 angleskee* (I can still co-pilot the TU-95 bomber)."

"Not until both your arm and leg are back to one hundred percent."

"Colonel Melnikoff, the casts came off three days ago. I am feeling fine."

It had been three weeks since she crashed in the desert.

He picked up a slip of yellow paper. "Not according

93

to the flight surgeon.”

“What does he know?” Sasha asked. “He has never set one foot in a cockpit.”

“No, but he had both feet in four years in medical college to learn you are still disabled.”

“Temporarily. If I do not fly, I do not live.”

“Then you can go to the control center at Vladivostok Airfield, to monitor air traffic over Safandel desert.”

“Why not just send me to the old pilots’ home?”

“My God, Sasha, do you ever do what you are told?”

She smiled at her commanding office. “If it suits me.”

The colonel dropped the yellow paper and picked up a white one. “Then maybe this will suit you.” He scanned down the document. “In three weeks’ time, a classified experimental aircraft will be delivered to this very facility. Do you want to test fly it or not?”

“Is it a jet?”

“No.”

“Prop?”

“No. And I will answer no more questions. Take it or leave it. Otherwise, you will be assigned to the academy to teach basic navigation to new recruits. At least that will get you out of my hair.”

“What is there besides jet and prop?”

“I said, no questions. Now, meantime, you are officially on vacation for two weeks. Go to Sochi, and lay in the sun.”

“Lay in the snow, you mean.” Sasha took out her phone and typed a short message.

“Well?”

She smiled. “I will let you know in one moment.”

Her phone chimed, and she checked the message.

"Give me permission to travel to St. Tropez," she said to the colonel, "for my two weeks of forced vacation, and upon my return I will accept this assignment for a not jet, not prop secret aircraft."

"Ha, the French Riviera?"

She nodded.

Colonel Melnikoff shook a cigarette from his Marlboro pack. "I am so glad you agree to follow orders. If your great grandfather was not General Secretary Leonid Ilyich Brezhnev, you would be sweeping my office floor instead of demanding the French Riviera." He lit up his smoke. "Now, get out of here."

She grabbed her purse from the floor and stood, reaching for the chair back to steady herself. "Thank you, sir." She popped a salute, then walked toward the door. Her phone chirped again.

"And be sure to perform your physical therapy exercises every day of those three weeks," he said.

She looked at her phone. "Yes, sir." She limped toward the door. "I already have my masseur scheduled for St. Tropez."

Chapter Eleven

Rigger brushed his finger down the face of his phone and touched the first number on the list. He took a coffee mug from the kitchen cabinet as he listened to the phone.

Pugsley answered on the third ring. "Hey, Rig, what's up?"

"Someone's been tailing me." Rigger poured steaming coffee into the mug. He told Pug about the tracks in the snow.

"Well, well," Pugsley said, "Raider's partner isn't too bright."

Rigger sipped his coffee. "You think that's who it is? The guy working with her?"

"Pretty sure. You and Wolf want to take a walk in the park?"

"We can do that. What time?"

"Gimme an hour to get set up, then walk past the statue of General Sherman. Make a circuit to Shakespeare, and back around Sherman again. That way, I'll be sure I'm shooting the right guy."

"Okay. Meet me back here afterward, and we'll decide what to do from there."

Rigger and Wolf performed as instructed, then returned to his apartment. At half-past twelve, Pugsley knocked at his door.

"Come in, Pug," Rigger said. "I've got the computer set up on the dining room table."

Thirty minutes later, Pugsley said, "Call Raider, and ask her over for dinner. Tell her I'm making lasagna and might need some help."

* * * * *

When Katrina and Rachel arrived that evening, Rigger let them in. Pugsley sat on the couch, facing the doorway. Rachel gave Rigger a hug, then ran to hug Pugsley. She then pulled out Wolf's box of toys and dumped them on the floor, ready for playtime.

Katrina sniffed the air. "You call that lasagna?" she said to Pugsley as she took off her coat and handed it to Rigger.

"I haven't started yet," Pugsley said, staring at her.

"Oh, you need my help, huh?"

"Yeah, I guess I do. But first I want you to see something on the computer."

The three of them went to the dining room, where the computer was still on the table. Rachel stayed behind to play with the puppy. Pugsley sat down and started the video as Katrina and Rigger stood on each side of him.

The movie began with Rigger and Wolf walking slowly past the statue of General Sherman. Two joggers ran by as Rigger and the dog went on along the path toward Shakespeare. Ten seconds behind Rigger came a man wearing a leather biker's jacket and ragged blue jeans. He was tall, maybe six-foot-four, slightly stoop-shouldered, and he smoked one of those small cigarette-sized cigars. The man slouched on along the path behind Rigger and Wolf, walking slowly but keeping his eyes on the path ahead. He occasionally pulled up his pants, using his

97

elbows.

Pugsley clicked the fast forward icon until Rigger and the puppy came back around the Sherman statue, then he slowed the video to regular speed. Soon the biker walked by, obviously following Rigger. The camera zoomed in on the man. His long, stringy hair hung down in his face. He flipped away the little cigar butt and spat into the snow at Sherman's feet. When he wiped his mouth on the back of his hand, Pugsley slowed the video as the man's head came around. He slowed it again and enlarged the image. The man, who appeared to be in his late twenties, faced directly toward the spot where Pugsley had hidden himself in a snowy thicket of young cedars, using his phone to record the video. Pugsley froze the frame.

Two of the man's front teeth were missing, one from the top, and one from the bottom. The tooth gaps didn't line up, and the remaining teeth were broken and yellow.

Rigger and Pugsley turned to Katrina. Neither of them spoke; their expressions were stony.

"What?" Katrina said, looking from Rigger to Pugsley. "You show me an exciting movie of Rigger and Wolf walking in the park, then some oddball who looks like First Runner-Up in New York's Ugliest Man contest. You two have got to find a new hobby."

"You know him," Rigger said. It wasn't a question.

"I hope not."

"He's been tailing Rigger," Pugsley said.

"Why?" she asked.

"You tell us?"

"How would I know."

"Come on, Cat," Pugsley said. "We know you don't live on the streets, and you don't work at Wellington Labs. You, or the other Katrina, have a degree in ethno...pharmo..."

"Pharmacological ethnobotany," Katrina said.

"See, that's what I mean. And you set up that begging-on-the-street bit for only one reason, to get your claws into Rigger. You know he's dying, and you're trying to set yourself—and your pal here—" he nodded to the computer screen, "as his beneficiary."

Her eyes went wide as she looked from Pugsley to Rigger. "Dying?" she whispered.

"And we know Rachel lives at St. Cecilia's Orphanage," Rigger said. "She's no relation to you."

Katrina seemed not to hear what Rigger said. She swallowed. "Dying?" Her lips formed the word, but no sound came out.

A scream came from Rigger's side. None of them had noticed Rachel coming up beside him. The picture of the biker was still on the computer screen.

The girl cried out and raised her hands in a shielding motion, between herself and the man. She tried to get away but ran into one of the chairs. She tumbled to the floor, then jumped up and ran for the stairs. The three adults followed her.

"Rachel!" Rigger yelled, trying to make himself heard over the girl's hysterical screaming.

She ran to the bedroom, where she and Katrina had slept the night before.

Rigger found her cowering behind the bed, crying and clutching her knees to her chest. He picked her up to hold her in his arms and sat on the bed.

"It's okay, baby," he said softly as he rocked her back and forth. "No one's going to hurt you."

"Mommy!" she cried. "Mommy, Mommy! Blood all on her face."

Katrina sat beside Rigger. "It's all right,

sweetheart," she said as she brushed the wet hair from the girl's cheek. "It's all over now."

Rachel still sobbed, but she began to calm down.

"When did you shoot that video?" Katrina whispered up to Pugsley.

"This morning."

She turned back to the girl. "I'm going downstairs to make some brown milk for you, Rachel. Are you going to be okay?"

The girl sniffed as she lay her head against Rigger's chest.

Downstairs in the kitchen, Katrina motioned toward the computer. "Run it again, from the beginning."

Pugsley sat at the computer and clicked on an icon to restart the video.

When the movie began, she took a slim wallet from the hip pocket of her jeans and handed it to Pugsley as she pulled him out of the chair. She sat in the chair and watched the movie intently.

Pugsley opened the wallet. He caught his breath, and his eyebrows went up. Curving around the shiny metal shield were the letters "N.Y.P.D. Detective 714. Homicide."

"You gotta be kidding me."

"I work undercover," she said, still watching the video. "Rigger was our last suspect in the murder of his wife and daughter, along with the murder of Rachel's parents."

"Was?"

"We also thought he might be involved in the disappearance of a girl about Rachel's age. She has blue eyes and blonde hair, just like Rachel."

"Was?" Pugsley asked again.

She looked up at Pugsley. "I know he couldn't kill anyone, Pug, but I didn't know that four weeks ago. How do you know he's dying?"

Pugsley explained about the brain disease.

"Is there no hope at all?" She took her police badge from him and slipped it into her hip pocket.

He shrugged and held out his hands in a helpless gesture. "He's had three doctors' opinions, all with the same prognosis."

"Pug." She took Pugsley's hand and held it tight. "I don't think I can handle this." She began to cry as she stood.

He pulled her close and wrapped his arms around her.

Katrina's shoulders shook as she sobbed against his chest.

Rigger came down the stairs, carrying Rachel. When he saw Katrina hanging onto Pugsley, and him with his arms around her, Rigger stopped on the steps, stunned by what he saw.

Before they noticed him, he took Rachel to the living room and sank down on the sofa, staring at the blank TV.

By 10:30, Rachel had fallen asleep on the love seat. Rigger told Pugsley and Katrina he felt worn out and a bit dizzy.

"You can let yourselves out," he said, then turned away and went to his bedroom.

* * * * *

The next day, Wednesday, the phone rang as Rigger and Wolf ate breakfast.

"Hi, Rig."

"Good morning, Katrina."

"Can Rachel and I come by to see you? I want to

101

talk to you about that Neanderthal who followed you through the park."

"I imagine Pugsley's down at the police department right now, talking to his pals about that guy. Better to leave serious stuff to professionals who know what they're doing."

"Professionals?"

"And anyway, I planned to go out to JFK at ten to see the B-17 Bomber."

"I think Rachel and I had better go out to the airport with you."

"Why?"

"If that guy's still on your tail, you may need protection."

"Protection by who? Rachel?"

A long silence passed before Katrina spoke. "Yeah, right. Rachel can protect you, and I'll just go along to learn her offensive tactics."

"You're talking really weird today, Katrina. I suppose you can go along if you want, but watching an old World War Two aircraft might be boring for you guys."

"It'll be fun."

"All right. I'll pick you up."

"No, don't do that. We'll come over to your place."

"Don't want me to see where you live, right?"

"It's just simpler if we come there."

"That's what I thought."

He clicked off the phone and tossed it onto the couch.

Chapter Twelve

Rigger stood behind the rope barricade with Katrina and Rachel, watching the B-17 taxi in from the runway and pull to a stop, fifty yards in front of them.

Four crewmen jumped from the World War II bomber and went through their routine of chocking the wheels and inspecting the aircraft. Soon they lined up in front of the wing, then the pilot and co-pilot dropped from a door in the belly of the plane. The four men came to attention, and one of them snapped a salute for the two officers. One officer returned the man's salute, and Rigger was surprised to see it was a young woman.

He and the other spectators applauded as the two came toward the rope to greet the sightseers.

Rigger gazed at the beautiful aircraft, hoping they'd allow people inside to see what it was like.

B-17 Bomber—Appearance - 10, Likability - 10, Attitude - 10, Usefulness - 0.

"I wonder if they'll let us go inside?" Katrina asked from beside him.

"That's exactly what I—"

"Rigger Entime?"

He was startled by the female voice. It was the

officer from the B-17.

"Yes," he said, puzzled about how she knew him. "Yes, I'm Rigger Entime."

She smiled and reached to shake his hand. "You couldn't possibly remember me. There were over a hundred students in that lecture hall the day you gave a talk on micromechanics."

"Which school?" He took her hand.

"MIT."

"Professor Chancellor's class. I remember a lot of good questions that day."

"I'm the one who asked about your gyroscope."

"Oh, yes. You wanted to know how the self-calibration worked."

"The class ended before you finished telling me about the miniature—"

Katrina cleared her throat, rather more loudly than necessary.

Rigger let go of the young woman's hand.

"I'm sorry," she said, holding out her hand to Katrina. "You must be Mrs. Entime."

"No," Rigger said. "She is not my wife."

Katrina laughed. "What a ridiculous idea. I just tag along behind him sometimes, hoping he'll trip over one of his tiny gyros. I'm Katrina Raider."

"Glad to meet you. I'm Autumn Willow." They shook hands. "And who's this pretty little girl?" Autumn knelt down, holding out her hand to the girl.

"Rachel," she said, taking Autumn's hand. "I'm in the Bible, you know."

"Oh, *that* Rachel. Well, I've read a lot about you."

"You have?"

"Yes. How would you like to see the inside of my airplane?"

Rachel held onto Autumn's hand and ducked under the rope. "Okay."

"Can I go, too?" Rigger asked.

"Well, I don't know," Autumn said. "What do you think, Rachel?"

Rachel glanced at Katrina and Rigger, wrinkling her brow and trying to look serious. After a moment, she grinned and nodded to Autumn.

When Rigger lifted the rope, Katrina ducked under. "You're not going anywhere without me."

"I never said I would."

Rigger heard grumbles of complaint from the other spectators.

Autumn must have heard them also, because she walked backward, still holding Rachel's hand. "Regular tours begin in ten minutes," she said to the crowd. She leaned down to Rachel and spoke in a lower voice, "My V.I.P. gets to go first."

"Yea!" Then after a moment, "What's V.I.P.?"

"Very Important Person."

Rachel looked to Katrina and Rigger. "I'm a very 'portant person."

"Yes, you are, sweetheart," Rigger said.

Katrina hurried to walk beside him. "What is your problem?" she asked in a loud whisper.

"I don't have a problem."

"You've been acting like a genuine ass all day."

"I'm not the one acting."

"Neither am I."

"Oh, this is the real Katrina, then?"

"Yes."

"Right. You've put on so many acts, I doubt you know who you are."

"I know who I am, but I don't know who you are

today."

"I'm the same dope who felt sorry for a woman begging for coins on the street."

"Haven't you talked to Pug about who I am?"

"How could I, with you two clenched together all the time? I'm surprised you came up for air long enough to call me this morning."

"You really are a saphead, you know that?"

The crew had placed a set of steps in the open bomb bay for easy access. By the time Rigger and Katrina came to the steps, Autumn and Rachel were already at the top, waiting. Rigger went up first, letting Katrina follow.

Autumn lifted the girl to her arms and walked toward the back of the aircraft.

"Wow!" Rachel exclaimed. "It's big in here."

"Beautiful," Rigger said when he came to stand beside Autumn.

"Everything is either original or reproduced from blueprints Grandfather received from the Boeing Corporation. They built the plane in 1943."

"Do these work?" Katrina asked. The four of them stood between the two fifty-caliber machine guns mounted in the middle of the aircraft.

"Yes. They're sometimes called waist guns. But we don't keep any ammo onboard."

"Too bad. I'd like to try one of 'em on someone."

"What about the electronics?" Rigger asked Autumn, while glaring at Katrina. "Is that all original, too?"

"It is, but we've added some modern avionics." Autumn looked from Rigger to Katrina, then back again. "We have a transponder, weather radar, and also a crash beacon."

"Do you ever get to fly the plane?" he asked.

"My grandfather's the pilot, and I'm the co-pilot.

But I fly it quite a bit."

"Can we see the cockpit?"

"Sure."

Autumn led the way toward the front of the plane. When they entered the navigator's cabin, she handed Rachel over to Katrina. Autumn slipped into the co-pilot's seat on the right and motioned for Rigger to sit in the pilot's seat.

"Holy smokes!" he said. "I've never seen so many instruments."

"Each of the four engines has several meters and gauges, in addition to the altimeter and airspeed indicator. Everything is duplicated for the pilot and co-pilot."

Rigger gazed in amazement at the impressive array of instrumentation.

Autumn turned her wheel, and Rigger's moved with hers. "The two wheels are cabled together, and they're used to work the ailerons. Look out your side window at the back side of the wing."

"Yes, I see the ailerons moving."

"Pulling the yoke back and forth works the elevator, and the pedals operate the rudder."

He watched her move the wheel and press the pedals with her feet.

"That's all there is to flying," she said.

Rigger lifted his feet to the pedals and put his hands on the wheel. He grinned as he worked the controls. "I guess you have to fishtail when you taxi, so you can see what's ahead of the aircraft."

Autumn stared at him, wrinkling her brow.

"I've got a private pilot's license. But for single engine only. Flying a Cessna 150 is child's play compared to this baby."

"My first solo was in my grandfather's Cessna 150."

"Did he cut your shirttail off?"

She reached to a pocket on the side of her seat, pulled out a book, and held it out to Rigger.

"Your logbook?"

He opened it, and inside the front cover was a cut-off piece of frilly pink fabric. Someone had written on her cut-off shirttail with a ballpoint pen, "Autumn Willow. First Solo flight. Wovenbridge Virginia. July 11, 2012."

"I was sixteen when Grandpa wrote that. He taught me to fly right after my ninth birthday."

"I guess you're about to get your bachelor's degree at MIT?"

"I'm a grad student, working on my master's."

"Really?"

She nodded.

"I'm working on a master's degree, too," Katrina chimed in.

"Are you?" Autumn said, looking up at the other woman where she stood between the seats. Katrina still held Rachel in her arms.

"Yes," Katrina replied. "Have you started on your thesis?"

"I'm about halfway. You?" Autumn twisted a curly red tendril around her finger, then slipped it over her ear.

"I've started on it, and I've collected a ton of information, but it's at a standstill until I can do some fieldwork. I want to compile an ethnopharmacopeia."

"'Pharm,' like pharmacology, 'copeia,' as in encyclopedia, and 'ethno' would be tribal. So I'm guessing it's a compilation of medicinal plants used by primitive tribes to cure ailments."

"Well, for goodness sakes, you are a quick one."

"Is there any particular tribe you're interested in?"

"From my studies so far, I'm leaning toward the

Yanomami."

"In the Amazon?"

Katrina nodded.

"Well, you'd definitely want the rainforest because of the thousands of plants. If you could go deep enough into the Amazon and find an old shaman who hasn't changed over to aspirin and penicillin, I bet you could learn a lot."

"Yeah, that would be cool."

"What's the subject of your thesis?" Rigger asked Autumn.

"Thermodynamics in quad-molecular fuel cells."

"I think that's been done," Katrina said.

Both Rigger and Autumn looked up at her.

"Kidding," she said with a grin, glancing from one unamused expression to the other. "Can't you ever take a joke, Entime?"

"Hello in the cockpit," someone said from behind Katrina.

"Hello," Autumn said.

"All the common people are clamoring to see the inside of the Shenandoah."

"Sorry, Grandpa. We got carried away."

"The Wingnuts are holding 'em back."

"What's a Wingnut?" Katrina asked.

"That's our crew," Autumn said. "Sherman Williams, Hanky Brubaker, Purdy Boy Boyd, and Wrongfoots Matthew Tull."

"Wrongfoots?"

"Yeah. It comes from someone trying to teach him the Tango when we were in Argentina."

Rigger and Autumn squeezed out of their seats and crowded into the navigator's cabin with Mr. Willow, Katrina and Rachel.

"Guess who this is, Grandpa?" Autumn said. "It's Mr. Entime."

"Rigger Entime?" Grandpa Willow reached to shake hands. "I'm glad to finally meet you. All I've heard for the past two years is about Rigger and his magic gyroscope, so small, a dozen would rattle around inside a thimble."

"Grandpa!" Autumn punched her grandfather in the shoulder.

"I'm Baylor Willow, and I taught this little scamp everything she knows, except micromechanics. She learned that on her own."

"Um," Katrina said. "Would you guys mind if we move this conversation outside? Someone's ego has inflated to such a size, it's got me shoved into a corner here."

"Me, too," Rachel said, rubbing the top of her head.

"I'm sorry," Autumn said. "Grandpa Willow, this is...um..."

"Katrina Raider," Katrina said. "I would shake your hand, but I don't know where mine is at the moment."

Mr. Willow laughed and turned to go out the doorway. "Here, let me take this little girl."

"She's Rachel," Autumn said. "From the Bible."

"No kidding," Mr. Willow said. "I've always wanted to meet you."

"Well, for goodness cakes. You know me, too?"

Grandpa Willow eased down the steps with Rachel, followed by Katrina. Rigger and Autumn stood in the open bomb bay, at the top of the steps, talking.

Finally, the two of them went down to join the others.

"We're going to be in New York for a while," Autumn said to Rigger. She took a business card from her breast pocket and handed it to him. "I'd like to buy you a cup of coffee sometime."

Rigger glanced at Katrina, who stood beside the steps, her arms folded, staring at him. "Sure," he said, reaching to take her card. "I'd like that, Autumn."

"You can call me 'Clicker.'"

"Okay. And I also want to hear more about the progress on your thesis. I'm working on a project in dire need of a tiny fuel cell."

Chapter Thirteen

South Bronx, New York

"When the parallel lines of your heart and spirit come together, you will no longer cast a shadow on this rock of human bondage called Earth."

The speaker paused to gaze around the poorly lighted room. As her narrowed eyes swept the roomful of malcontents, social misfits, and other human debris, she occasionally hesitated to hold a man with her piercing stare.

Angelgrace Casperian, thirty-eight years old, barely five feet tall, skinny and gaunt, reminiscent of a concentration camp survivor. But her voice was deep and mellow, like a cathedral bell at sunset. Her black hair hung in dreads and random braids, dropping to the middle of her back and over her eyes. Pale and sallow, she appeared sickly, but her Pacific eyes flashed with fire and hatred.

Two blocks off 34th Street, in the South Bronx, she stood at a small podium in a smoky room filled with human debris.

"Your lifetime will coalesce..." she flipped her head to the side to shake the hair from her eyes and lifted her right hand toward the ceiling, palm outward, fingers outstretched, "to a quivering point..." she clenched her fist and brought it down on the podium, "and vanish forever." She gripped the side edges of the podium with both hands, leaned forward, and hissed, "Forever," sounding a reverberating echo. "Leaving not even a lousy period at the end of your life sentence."

Angelgrace looked around the audience, seeing a few of the men nod in agreement. Her eyes then lit on the only woman present. She was young, maybe twenty-five, her blonde hair cropped short, and she wore new army camos, tailored for a snug fit. Angelgrace stared at her and spoke.

"What about my flesh and bones, you might ask." The young woman blinked and glanced down at her lap.

A half-dozen more men came in the door and stood at the back of the room. They wore identical black jackets over brown shirts. All six were trim and fit, with an almost military bearing. Angelgrace smiled and looked toward the fat Jamaican leaning against a wall, beyond the end of the stage. He nodded, gave her a slow blink, and champed his cigar.

"Your body is ninety-seven percent water. The rest is organic minerals, except for the fillings in your teeth. A hundred years from now, everyone in this room will have dissolved back into the earth, except for those fillings. They'll lie around for ten thousand years until some misguided archeologist from a tiny planet orbiting Alpha Centauri comes to dig them up and marvel at such wonders left by the extinct creatures who once lived here."

She waited for the few chuckles to die down. "There's nothing beyond this confinement. If you intend to make a mark on eternity, make it now. For evil, for vengeance, or for pure hatred, make your mark now. And know this; it's better to be remembered for a heinous crime than not remembered at all."

Angelgrace took up her glass of water and drank, watching the gathering of societal dregs. A drop of water ran from the corner of her mouth and down her chin. A scraggly-bearded man with no teeth coughed and scratched his chest. She glared at him and replaced her glass on the podium, then wiped the back of her hand over her chin and down her throat, across the stained-glass tattoo encircling her neck.

"You think they'll chisel into your tombstone, 'Here lies Calvin Don Ronishard...'"

When she paused, a man sitting cross-legged on the floor behind her jerked up his head at the sound of his name.

"'He helped an old lady across the street'? Hell yes, they will. But who's going to read it? There are slave graveyards in the woods all over the South nobody even knows about. Kudzu and poison ivy cover their stones and bones. Are you going down there to see what's cut into their headstones? No, and I ain't either."

She paused to watch a young man in overalls and long, ratty hair light a hand-rolled cigarette. He inhaled deeply and held it while returning her icy stare.

"But what if they were to chisel into the history books, 'Here lies Calvin "The Chopper" Ronishard, he butchered a crippled old nun in the middle of Broadway, then hacked her head off with a claw-hammer while all the sheep in human clothing bleated and watched the red runoff with fear and fascination?'

"John Wayne Gacy's idiotic painting of a clown sold for five hundred dollars last month. You know why?"

A man in the front row shook his head while keeping his one remaining eye on the woman before him.

"Was it because Gacy studied the school of Botticelli, or the school of Raphael? No, his childish art sells because he sucked the life out of thirty-two boys, then buried the leftover pieces of their bodies he didn't eat under his floorboards.

"Does anyone here remember Raymond Tillen, Walter J. MacDaren, or Barbara K. Winsome?"

Her eyes roved the audience. She waited. Some people looked around at the others. A few shook their heads.

"Of course you don't. Those three people were carried out the back door of the Shady Hollow Retirement Center last evening and hauled down to the city morgue. How about James Earl Ray, Lee Harvey Oswald, and Sirhan Sirhan?"

Several people murmured, then one man said, "Yeah, I know all of 'em"

"They were nobody," Angelgrace said. "Just three gutless Republican bastards until they murdered Martin Luther King, Jr., John F. Kennedy, and Bobby Kennedy. Now they get nearly the same number of hits on Google as the men they killed, exceeded only by Adolph Hitler. That's how you make your mark in this empty-headed, God-fearing world. Carve your name in human flesh.

"In the end, the old folks' home will process the cowards, while the brave go to the gallows and become famous." She paused to let her words take hold. "Your tombstone is already sitting in the warehouse..." she pointed at a man in a worn-out field jacket and black stocking cap, who fidgeted under the attention she drew to him, "just waiting for an epitaph. So go out tonight, my children..." she released the pitiful man from her pointing finger, "and make your mark on the landscape of humanity. Give them something to remember. Give all those stinking Republican bloodsuckers up there something to piss and moan about. And don't let them take you to a rest home, where you'll fade away in ignominious anonymity. Chisel your own epitaph, and make it bold and cold." She glanced around the room and waited. "Tonight!" she shouted. "The Earth is already pregnant with fire!"

She turned abruptly and left the podium. After a moment, the audience began to clap for Angelgrace Casperian. It wasn't exactly a standing ovation, but it was a pretty good round of applause.

"Heap of fuckin' worthless sons-a-bitches," she whispered.

"Who is, Gracie? Who's the sons-a-bitches?" Calvin asked, flitting at her side.

"All of 'em, Calvin Don. Every last one of those rotten bastards, and that one phony bitch in tailored camos, too. Who the hell does she think she's fooling? She couldn't chase down a three-legged dog on a Harley Hog." Angelgrace walked toward the Jamaican man, who now stood by the back door. "She's definitely another fuckin' Republican spy. If I see her hanging around again, I'll kick her ass so hard, she'll have to unbutton her collar to take a piss."

"I know it, Gracie," Calvin said, apparently still mulling over her previous statement. "They really are sons-a-bitches. But not me, right Gracie? I know about that ignoramus stuff you told about. I 'member it from last time you talked. And the slave stones and bones, they're down there in the woods with poison stuff all over them, huh Gracie?" Calvin hitched up his trousers with his elbows and fell in behind her, stepping on her heel.

"Goddamnit, Calvin." She turned on him. "Didn't I

tell you not to walk on my fuckin' heel?" Angelgrace glared up at him, her fists on her hips. She lifted her foot behind her to pull the laceless waffle-stomper back on her left foot. The other foot, the metal one, was fitted with a black brogan. "You don't have to be right on my fuckin' ass all the time." She dropped her foot back to the floor and made a quick movement with her hand.

Calvin cringed, both hands flying up to shield his face.

She belayed her intention to punch him and instead reached to fix the undone button of his broad chest, just above her eye level.

He watched this act of kindness from between his shaking fingers.

"I know, Gracie." Calvin shoved his hands into his pockets and immediately pulled them out to hitch up his trousers with his elbows. "You did tell me not to follow so close on your fuckin' ass. You told me that before. And I ain't never gonna do that again. Never will."

"Come on," she said. "Let's get the hell outta here."

Calvin stepped on her heel again.

"Shit!" She kicked backward, hard, with her metal foot, catching Calvin on the shin. "Gimme my stuff, Bustamante," she said to the Jamaican. "I gotta get out of this stinking rat hole."

Bustamante handed her a new hundred-dollar bill, folded into a hexagram, a shape sometimes called the King's Star by astrologers. A bit of white power leaked from one of the six points.

"See ya Wednesday night, Angelface," the fat old man growled around his soggy cigar butt. His hanging jowls were covered with a three-day splotchy gray stubble.

She flipped her head to the side, clearing a lock of black hair from her eyes, and glared up at him. "The hell you will." She felt the heft of the folded bill, then slipped it into her shirt pocket, pressing it against her unrestrained pubescent-sized breast. "And it's Angelgrace, you numbskull."

He grinned.

"You see that skinny bitch in camos?" she asked him.

"Yeah, I know her. She's good. Wants to be a member."

Angelgrace blew a puff of air from her nose, then she and Calvin walked outside into the icy winter night. She stopped in the cold flicker of a street lamp to light a cigarette. When she got it going, she held up the burning match to Calvin's face.

"What the hell are you crying about now?" Smoke puffed out around her words.

Calvin only shook his head and wiped his nose on a sleeve.

She reached up to put her hand on his stooped shoulder and turned him away from the light. They walked toward a beat-up '73 Chevy Malibu parked on the wrong side of the deserted street.

"You got Ike in your pocket?" she whispered.

Calvin nodded and grinned.

Chapter Fourteen

At midmorning, Rigger dialed the number on Autumn's card. She answered on the third ring.

"Remember that offer you made me?" he asked.

"Well, that was yesterday. I have a good memory, but it's short, and I make so many offers, you'll have to remind me exactly what I offered you."

Rigger laughed. "Instead of coffee, how about a little lunch?"

"How about a lot of little lunches? I'm starving."

"Oh, what a sweet-talker you are."

"I'm sweet to anyone who gives me food."

"Um...I thought you were buying?" Rigger said.

"Oh, you're talking about *that* offer. Maybe some other time, then." She laughed. "What time, where, and I hope it's casual?"

"Shorts and tees are the uniform of the day."

"Cool."

They decided on a time, and Rigger asked the name of the hotel where she stayed. Two hours later, they sat in a cozy little café on Lafayette Street in Soho, sharing a large pizza, along with a pitcher of beer. When she sloughed out of her fluffy scarf-coat, she really did wear a tee shirt and shorts.

"You're not a spy, are you, Autumn?" Rigger filled her glass from the beer pitcher.

"It's 'Clicker,' and I might be. You have anything I can spy on?"

"Clicker. Where did you get a nickname like that?"

She explained about the telegraph key her grandfather had given her when she was a kid, and how she clicked away on it so much, he began calling her 'Clicker.'

"Your grandpa seems like a pretty nice guy."

"Yeah, I don't know what I'd do without him. I never knew my mother and father, so Grandpa has always been my dad."

"Where you guys taking the B-17 from here?"

"Grandpa may put it in the hangar for the rest of the winter. All four engines are about due for major overhauls, and one of them keeps acting up. Brubaker and Wrongfoots are checking it out today to see if we have to call off the rest of the tour. If they think the engine's okay, then we're on our way to Chicago, Oklahoma City, Dallas, and Austin. I'd like to finish the tour before I go back to school. Why do you think I'm a spy?"

Rigger studied her face while chewing a bite of pizza. She sipped her beer. He wiped his mouth on a napkin and took a drink.

"The military project I'm working is classified top secret."

"Oooo." Autumn leaned forward. "Tell me more, and talk into my...um...fork here, if you don't mind."

"Cute. But listen, I have two problems I can't solve."

"What is this thing we're talking about? A spaceship? A nuclear cannon?"

"No, nothing like that. It's a tiny drone aircraft, called the Dragonfly."

Autumn's face lit up. "Now you have my undivided attention. You said two things that top my list of all the wonderful words—tiny and aircraft. I'm hoping it's called the Dragonfly for a good reason."

"Yes. It's the size and shape of a real dragonfly. The theory is, no one will pay any attention to a dragonfly fluttering around a missile site or military convoy."

"What's the range on this little squirt?"

Rigger cleared his throat and carefully folded his napkin. "Approximately twenty-four inches."

Autumn laughed. "Not a whole lot of secret stuff lying around two feet from your home base, is there?"

"No, of course not. With the tiny video camera and microphone on board, it can't lift any additional weight, including its own battery. So, right now I have it attached to its power supply by two thin wires. I can fly it out two feet, but then the weight of the wires pull it down."

"What kind of controls does it have?"

"That's the second problem. My part of this project is the navigation system. The aerodynamics were designed by one group of engineers, and the flight control by another. It actually flies pretty well, but the controls are clunky. The aircraft has two sets of wings, and they flutter, almost exactly like a real dragonfly. The front pair of wings control forward and backward motion, and the rear pair move the craft up and down. Used in combination, you can bank left and right. The problem is, the flight control guys designed it with two joysticks, and you have to work them in coordination. I crashed that poor critter about a dozen times before I could even get it to hover above the tabletop."

"Wow." She sipped her beer, staring at Rigger over the rim of her glass.

"And that's with me having the Dragonfly in front

of me, where I can see it. When it goes on a mission, all the pilot at headquarters will have for reference is the video sweep ahead of him.”

“What kind of battery you running it on?”

“One triple A battery.”

“Hmm...that’s like one in a TV remote control, pretty small. What size battery is that, a volt and a half?”

Rigger nodded.

“If you didn’t have the wires attached to the Dragonfly, how long would it fly on a volt and a half-power source?”

“About an hour.”

“Is that long enough to do any good?”

“It’ll have to do for now. And that’s if we can even get that small amount of power on board the aircraft. That’s why I’m interested in your work on quad-molecular power cells.”

“Any practical use of those power cells is years away. It’s all purely theoretical right now.”

“I’ve only got a year...” Rigger unfolded and refolded his napkin. He wadded it up and tossed it onto his empty plate. “Maybe less.”

“Is there anything on the Dragonfly that isn’t absolutely essential? Any item that can be jettisoned?”

“Well, obviously it has to have the video camera and the microphone. The only other item onboard is an incendiary device. They don’t intend for the aircraft to fall into the wrong hands.”

“How much does that weigh?”

“An ounce, maybe an ounce and a quarter.”

Rigger watched Autumn narrow her eyes on him. He saw her glance at his chin, then his shoulders. Her eyes wandered to his chest, up to his lips, and finally back to his eyes.

"Is there a drug store around here?" she asked.

"Probably."

"Let's go." She drained her glass and scooted away from the table. "I need something from the drugstore."

Chapter Fifteen

Rigger and Autumn found a drugstore three blocks from the café. When they walked in, the lady behind the counter gave them a quick once-over; apparently satisfied they weren't going to rob or rape her, she licked a thumb and turned the page of her National Enquirer.

Autumn looked around the store, then stepped to the counter. Rigger followed. As they stood watching the woman for a moment, she flipped another page of her magazine.

"Excuse me," Autumn said.

The woman moved in slow motion, looking first toward Autumn, then to Rigger. She glanced back at Autumn, raising her eyebrows—a New Yorker's way of saying, "You want something from me?"

"Do you have hearing aid batteries?"

The lady was in her mid-forties, overweight by a hundred and fifty pounds, and wore orange eye shadow with pink rouge and a yellow Hawaiian muumuu with huge red flowers. She almost smiled and reached for the eyeglasses dangling on a gold chain around her neck. She slipped them on and gave Rigger another look through hugely magnified eyes.

"What model ya got, kid?" This was also done in slow motion, as if her jaws were tired from a hard day of chewing. She slurred her words the way a teen does to irritate her parents. About halfway through "moooodel," she tilted her head to peer at Autumn's left ear.

"What model what?" Autumn tilted her head to match the woman's.

The lady exhaled through her nose, as if trying to dislodge something that shouldn't be lodged there. "Ya want hearing aid batteries, or don't cha?"

"Yes," Autumn said.

"Then tell me the model of your frigging aid."

"I don't have a hearing aid."

"Get outta here. I ain't got no time for this kinda crap." These words came out like machinegun slugs.

"Look," Autumn said, "all I want is to see the smallest hearing aid battery you have."

"Why?"

Autumn leaned over the counter and whispered, "Because we're working on a secret project for the Pentagon and we need a tiny battery to fly a tiny airplane."

The woman stared at Autumn for a moment, then burst into a laughing fit.

Rigger lifted the flap on his shirt pocket, took out some folded currency, then peeled off a twenty-dollar bill and laid it on the counter.

The woman, still giggling, snatched the twenty. "Money talks, and you just spoke my language. Hearing aid batteries are on the rack at the end of the counter." She jerked a thumb to her right and picked up the magazine. "You can take your pick," she mumbled, making it sound more like, "Ya talkin' prick."

Autumn opened her mouth, but Rigger pushed her away, toward the end of the counter.

He rotated a circular rack with its large collection of NiCd hearing aid and watch batteries.

"How about this?" Autumn asked, lifting a pack of five tiny batteries, each about half the size of a pencil eraser.

Rigger took the package and squinted at the fine print. "One-point-four volts," he read. "Perfect. Let's go." He turned for the door.

"Wait a minute."

He looked back at her.

"Those cost only eight ninety-five for the whole pack," she whispered.

He shrugged.

"You gave her a twenty."

Another shrug. "Let's go."

Autumn grabbed a second pack of five batteries, glanced at the woman who continued to devour her magazine, then took another pack, this one containing two large watch batteries. She hurried to catch Rigger where he stood by the open door.

"Thanks," Autumn called to the woman.

She tilted up her head, almost half an inch. Maybe it was her way of saying, "Don't mention it." But she kept her eyes on an article about the Pentagon hiring outer space aliens to work inside nuclear power plants.

Autumn and Rigger were in his Jaguar and back on Broadway, heading for his apartment house. "You know there were security cameras all over that place."

"Yeah, and let that be a lesson to them. A thief could have walked out with half the store, and Ms. Mumbles wouldn't know it till dinner time."

When they got to his apartment, he pushed open the door and motioned her inside.

"Wow!" She walked across the room, taking in the

artwork and plush furniture, then went up the three steps to the raised living room. "Let's see the view."

Rigger pushed a button on the wall, parting the curtains.

Autumn slipped out of her jacket and tossed it on the couch. "Beautiful."

"It's okay."

"It's okay?" Autumn said. "A million dollar apartment with a ten million dollar view of Central Park, and you say, 'It's okay?'"

"Yeah. Come on, I'll show you something really pretty."

He led the way up the stairs and down the hall to the locked door. He slipped a key into the slot, unlocked it, then licked his finger and pressed it to an electronic pad built into the door. The door clicked and opened an inch.

"Did you just open a door with spit?"

"DNA, actually."

"Really?" Autumn walked into the dark room.

Rigger stepped in behind her, closing the door.

"What the heck?" She walked toward a wall of glass, stretching sixteen feet long.

He followed, waiting for her reaction.

"If I didn't know better..." she reached to touch the thick glass, "I'd think this is an eight-foot-tall rain forest habitat."

"Uh-huh."

The bottom one-third was filled with murky water, along with an assortment of slime-covered rocks, rotting logs, and several palm-sized fish swimming in lazy circles. In the back, the water lapped upon a muddy riverbank covered with tropical plants—ferns, miniature banana trees, and poinciana, along with a variety of carnivorous plants, such as Venus flytrap and honeydew. She also saw three types of orchids. Small mangroves grew along the water edge, and lily pads floated on the surface.

The habitat was lighted from above by a series of time-actuated lights, glowing from dim dawn to bright midday to faint dusk, then going dark for eight hours.

Two signs were planted on the far bank of the small pound.

"No swimming," Autumn read. "Don't pet the frogs." She knelt to get a better look at the fish. "Why no swimming? Is that meant for people, or the fish?"

Rigger went to a refrigerator and took out something wrapped in white paper. He brought it to the center of the glass, handed it to Autumn, then dragged a stepladder over from the corner of the room.

Autumn unwrapped the package. "Yum, raw meat."

"Go up the ladder, and you'll find a trapdoor on top."

She climbed up.

"Now, mind the frog sign, open the door, and drop the meat into the water."

When she dropped the meat, she started down the ladder, but before she reached the bottom, the surface of the water erupted in a feeding frenzy.

Rigger was on his knees, watching.

She knelt beside him. "Piranha," she whispered.

He nodded.

The half-pound of beef was gone in twenty seconds.

"Wow. Okay, I get the no swimming. But I don't see any cute little frogs to pet."

He fetched a glass container from the side of the room.

"Termites." She held the container to the light.

"Yes. Go back up and scatter a handful on the riverbank. And be sure to close the trapdoor."

"Yeah, guess you don't want any hungry piranha running around out here."

"It's not them I'm worried about."

She gave him a look, then went up the ladder. After tossing some termites on the riverbank, she closed the trapdoor and came down.

They watched the termites wiggling around, looking for a tasty rotten log.

Suddenly, a streak of blue came from the foliage, and a bright blue frog landed amid the bugs. As he began tonguing up the termites, another blue frog hopped in for a snack, then another.

"They're beautiful. Why can't I pet them?"

"The Yanomami call them poison dart frogs for a good reason. If they're frightened or agitated, they secrete an oily foam on their back. One touch, and your life is over in three minutes."

"Okay. No swimming, and no petting. I'm beginning to worry about you, Rigger."

"As well you should. Now come on, and I'll show you something really exciting."

"Hmm...more exciting than woman-eating fish and man-killing frogs?"

"Right." He flipped a switch on the wall.

Two lamps on a long worktable came to life. The lamps sat on either side of a square of black velvet, illuminating a small object in the center of the thick cloth.

Autumn went slowly to the table, knelt at the side, and gazed upon the Dragonfly. She didn't speak; only stared at the tiny aircraft.

Rigger stepped around to the other side and pulled up a wheeled stool. He watched Autumn reach out, but then she stopped and glanced up at him.

"You can touch it."

"It's not covered in frog foam?"

He grinned.

She slipped her fingers under the Dragonfly and lifted it, mindful of the two wires running across the velvet to a triple-A battery.

The Dragonfly was an inch-and-a-half long, with a two-inch wingspan. The four wings were covered with a transparent ultra thin Mylar.

"You can see the skeleton of the wings right through the fabric," Autumn whispered. "What are the struts made of?"

"I split matchsticks under my microscope." He motioned toward the other side of the room.

Autumn looked that way to see another bench running the length of the room. She saw a microscope, small metal lathe, and several soldering irons, along with a complete set of tiny power tools.

"After I split the matchsticks eight times, I bow the slivers of wood for strength and cement them in place using quick-dry glue applied with the tip of a needle."

She looked up at him, then carefully turned the Dragonfly to admire it from the front.

"It takes hours to repair a wing after I crash."

Two lenses were in the front where the eyes of a real dragonfly would be. An almost microscopic microphone was nestled below and between the lenses.

"Two cameras?" she asked.

"Yes, for stereoscopic vision." Rigger went to his notebook computer at the end of the table, brushed a fingertip across the screen, then turned the computer toward her. "The transmitter onboard the aircraft sends a digital signal back to the receiver." He pointed to a black box sitting at the opposite end of the table. "The receiver unscrambles and amplifies the signal, then sends it to my notebook computer.”

When the computer came on, Rigger used the touch pad and clicked a couple times. The screen went black. He flipped a switch on the receiver and moved one of the lamps toward Autumn, and a grainy image of her face materialized on the screen.

“Cool.” She rotated the Dragonfly to examine the rear section, and Rigger’s face appeared on the screen. She ran a finger along the back part.

“On an actual dragonfly, that would be the abdomen, but on this one, it’s our antenna. Set it back on the pad, and I’ll show you something.”

Six stiff wires, the width of spider web silk, extended down from the belly of the craft and splayed out. They were bent at an angle near the end.

“Nice landing gear.” Autumn set it down.

Rigger had painted green bars across the wings and brown markings on the antenna to imitate the segments on a real dragonfly’s abdomen. From a few feet away, except for the two wires coming from its belly, it looked like the real thing.

Rigger moved two joysticks and a small touchpad over in front of him. He licked his finger, touched the pad, then picked up the Dragonfly. He held the head of the aircraft close to his right eye while pressing a button on the right joystick. The Dragonfly blinked a tiny beam of red light into his eye, then beeped twice.

“Okay, it still loves me.” He replaced the aircraft on the mat.

“You’re sort of obsessed with security, aren’t you?”

“Sort of.”

He pressed a button on the left joystick and eased the other stick forward. A gentle hum came from the Dragonfly as the wings began to flutter. He tilted the first stick ever so slightly, and the Dragonfly lifted off the pad. A little pressure on the other stick caused the tiny aircraft to rotate in a complete circle, coming back to face Autumn.

"It's alive, Igor!" she whispered. "It's alive."

He flew the aircraft higher until it pulled its battery wires tight.

Autumn reached for the battery and lifted it to give the wires some slack. The aircraft flew higher. She eased off her knees and stood to follow the Dragonfly, while Rigger used the two joysticks to fly it around the room. After two circuits, he flew it back to the pad and hovered down to a smooth six-point landing. Autumn put down the battery and leaned on her elbows to gaze at the Dragonfly.

Rigger cut the power, and the wings fluttered to a stop.

"I always thought," Autumn said, "when I fell in love, it would be with a handsome jet jockey. But I'm in love, Rigger. For the first time, I'm truly in love. This has got to be the most wonderful little creature I've ever seen in my whole life."

"I kinda like it myself."

"My turn." She walked around the table.

"Let's try one of the new batteries first."

"Oh, yeah, I forgot."

While Rigger struggled to open the plastic pack containing the hearing aid batteries, Autumn went to the work bench and picked up the tiniest of the four soldering irons. She found a roll of thin solder on a shelf and went back to the worktable, where she plugged the iron into an electrical outlet on the table.

Rigger growled and ripped apart the plastic pack, scattering the tiny batteries across the velvet pad.

"You know there's a tab on the back of the package where you remove the batteries one at a time."

“Now you tell me.”

He snipped the wires close to the belly of the aircraft and stripped off the insulation. When the iron was hot, he held the battery with a pair of needle-nose pliers with red plastic tips, while Autumn soldered the wires to the battery—one on top, and one on the bottom.

He sat the aircraft, with the new battery held snugly against its abdomen, on the black pad. The two of them leaned down to gaze at it.

“Hmm...” Autumn said. “I think your Dragonfly’s pregnant.”

“It better not be. His name is Donovan.”

Autumn laughed. “Now can I take Donovan Dragonfly for a spin?”

“Sure. Just don’t forget, those joysticks are tricky.”

“You realize you’re talking to a flying ace here.” She gave him a grin.

He set the pair of joysticks in front of her. “Now, press this stick forward to increase the speed, and move it left and right to go up or down. On the other stick, you move it forward or backward to maneuver.”

“Sounds easy.”

“Yeah, well, it’s not. It takes lots of practice to get a feel for it.”

“You worry too much.”

“I know. All right, when you’re ready, press that button to start the engine.”

“Right, here we go.”

Autumn pressed the button, but nothing happened. “What?” She tried the button again. “Oh, I gotta look Donovan in the eye.” She picked him up and held him, as she’d seen Rigger do it; still no reaction from the Dragonfly.

“Good,” he said. “My security system works. Come

133

over here by the computer."

She stepped over beside him as he opened a small foil pack and took out a Clorox wipe.

"I hope you're going to clean off your spit before I touch it."

"Yep." He cleaned the touchpad.

"Now, a lick and a touch, Madam."

She did.

"Right eyeball here." He pointed to the computer's camera. "Two inches away, no blink."

She stared into the camera as he tapped the computer's touchpad.

"I'm setting your DNA and retina map to evaporate in twenty-four hours." His computer played the first eight bars of Beethoven's 'Für Elise,' and he responded with the next eight bars, using the keyboard. It then beeped twice. "If you behave, I might make it permanent."

"Gee, thanks, Papa."

"Okay, you know the drill. Let's see if you really are a pilot."

She went through the two security steps, bringing a quick two beeps from Donovan.

"Aw, he loves me, too." She pressed the controller button, and the Dragonfly's wings buzzed. "Why the red light when I look into his camera?"

"That makes your pupil dilate. That way, he knows your eyeball is alive, and not cut out of your dead body. Also, your finger temp has to be about ninety-eight-point-six, for the same reason."

"You should work for the CIA."

"Funny you should say that."

"You kidding me?"

"Never mind."

Autumn eased forward on her left joystick, and the

aircraft lifted off the pad. "Cool." She moved the right stick forward, and the Dragonfly veered off to the left, flying straight into the lamp. "Oh, shit!"

Rigger groaned and reached to cut the power. The aircraft fell to the pad, its two left wings still smoldering from contact with the hot light bulb.

Autumn—Appearance - 10, Likability - 10, Attitude - 10, Usefulness - 0.

She picked up the wounded Dragonfly and held it in the palm of her hand. "You should've told me those controls were so darn touchy." She gave him a mischievous smile.

Rigger wanted to be mad at her, but he couldn't. He'd crashed the plane at least a dozen times before he got the hang of flying it.

Dragonfly—Appearance - 10, Likability - 10, Attitude - 8, Usefulness – 0.

"Yeah," he said. "Well, guess who's going to spend the next three hours repairing those broken wings?"

"Um...that ethnobotics woman you took to the airport?"

"Very funny. Her name is Katrina, and I like her very much."

"Love her, you mean."

Rigger brought the microscope over to the worktable and poured out a box of matches. "I don't think so."

"I know so, just like everyone else at the airport knew it. You two were going on like a married couple."

"Really?"

Autumn nodded. She flipped on the microscope's light, put a matchstick under the lens, bent to the eyepiece, and held out her hand to him, palm up. "Scalpel."

Chapter Sixteen

Four days after Rigger and Katrina met Autumn at the B-17, Katrina was called into Captain Billingsly's office at police headquarters.

"You're off the case," the captain said.

"What?" Katrina asked.

"You're too close to it. You know better than to get involved with a suspect in a case you're assigned to."

"But Captain Billingsly," Katrina pressed the palms of her hands on his desk as she leaned forward, "Rigger is no longer a suspect."

"You illustrate my point for me. He's not a suspect as far as you're concerned, but to me he is."

"Why?"

"Does he have an alibi for each of the killings?"

"He does for last night."

"Where was he?"

"He was with me." Katrina sat down, folding her arms below her breasts, and fixed the captain with her cold stare.

"Report to Murphy. You're assigned to the Palanski

murder." Captain Billingsly wrote something on a form, slipped it into a file folder, and tossed it into his "Out" basket.

"Palanski? That's the gay lover's triangle case."

"Right."

Katrina stared at the floor, at the trashcan, then at the window. "That case is almost closed. They got the killer."

"Yeah, but there's paperwork to be done before it goes to trial."

"You're making me a clerk?"

"Keep it up, and you'll be writing parking tickets in Hell's Kitchen."

"Why don't you just fire me and be done with it?"

* * * * *

The doorbell chimed. Rigger went to answer it, but since it was late, he glanced through the peephole to see who was there before opening the door.

"Come in, Pug." He hurried back to the living room. "I want to see the rest of the news."

Pugsley closed the door and followed Rigger up the steps to the living area.

"There's been another double homicide." Rigger waved Pug to have a seat. The two of them watched the end of the newscast.

"I heard about it on the car radio. I wonder if it's part of Katrina's case?"

"What?"

"The M.O. is similar."

"What M.O.? And what case? Is she pretending to be a reporter now? And I'm surprised she's not with you."

Pugsley stared at Rigger, obviously perplexed by his friend's attitude. "Why would she be with me?"

Rigger clicked off the TV. "After the other night, I figured you two would be shacked up by now."

"Wait a minute—who are you, and what have you done with Rigger Entime?"

"Stop evading the issue. First you suspect Katrina is trying to get her hooks into me, then both of you take sides against me."

"Where did all this come from? Did you go to see your doctor today? Did you take your meds?"

"I don't need a doctor. I know what I saw."

"What did you see?" Pugsley asked.

"When I came down the stairs Tuesday evening, after Rachel's reaction to that guy on the video, the one you made in the park, I saw you and Katrina loving it up in the kitchen."

"Loving it up?! What the heck does that mean?"

"You were in each other's arms. And don't even try to deny it. My brain's not that far gone."

Pugsley grinned and chuckled. "Holy smokes, I can't believe it." He began to laugh.

"I'm glad you're able to see the humor, because I don't see a damn thing funny about it."

After a moment, Pugsley calmed down, but he struggled to keep from laughing. "Rigger, ole pal, I have some sad news for you."

"Okay, here it comes. More bull about Katrina's acting career."

"My friend, you're in love."

Rigger eyed him, wrinkling his brow. "That's the second time I've heard that today."

"And it's about time, too."

"You've gone off your rocker."

"Have you talked to Katrina since Tuesday night?" Pug asked.

"I don't know if I'd call it talking. She went to the airport with me yesterday, and the two of us, shall we say, exchanged words."

"Did you happen to see that little wallet she carries in her hip pocket?"

"Why would I want to see her wallet?"

"So, you don't know who she is?"

"She doesn't even know who she is," Rigger said.

"But I bet she tried to tell you, didn't she?"

"She went on about protecting me from the guy on my tail, and I asked her if that was another of her playacting roles."

"Oh, boy. Let's back up to the loving it up part," Pugsley said. "No, I'll have to go back more than that. You and I thought she was after your money and she'd probably planned to worm her way into your life to set herself up to be your beneficiary, right?"

"Right."

"Wrong. Prepare yourself for a shock, young man. She's an undercover cop working out of the homicide division of the NYPD."

"How do you know that?"

"Remember that little wallet? That's her detective's badge. She showed it to me Tuesday night, just before she went to pieces. I checked with Sergeant Robolinski. He didn't know about undercover, but she's definitely a homicide detective."

Rigger slumped back into the couch. "Went to pieces?"

"Yeah, now we come to the loving it up part. When a woman learns the man she cares about is dying, what's a good ole pal of yours to do? She needed a shoulder to cry on, and mine was the only one available. Until you so indelicately brought it up that night, she had no idea about the brain disease. Has anyone ever told you you're a sap?"

"Yes, I've heard that word applied to me several times."

"I'm not surprised. Katrina is crazy about you, and apparently you feel the same way about her. I just hope we can repair any damage you've done."

"I..." Rigger was lost for words. He thought back over the events of the past few days. "She's an undercover detective." He stared at the blank TV screen. "That explains everything. I *am* a sap."

"Right on all counts. She's assigned to the murder investigation of your family, and the murder of Rachel's parents. You were their last suspect. But now she's cleared you of any suspicion. That's why I wondered if she's working this new homicide. It's almost the same—a young man and woman butchered in a parking lot."

"I suppose she has a cellphone."

Pugsley nodded.

"And you probably have the number."

Pugsley took out his phone and clicked to the directory. "You ready?"

Rigger picked up the phone from an end table. "Okay, read it off." After he added Katrina's number to his directory, he called her.

Someone answered, "Yeah?"

"Is this Detective Raider?"

"Rigger?"

"Yes, and I'm ready for you to slap me around for being an idiot."

"You must've talked to Pug."

"He told me about your badge, and everything else."

"Pug's one of the good guys."

"I know you're probably working this new double-homicide case, but I'd like to see you when you get a break."

"I ain't working the new homicide."

"But I thought it has the same M.O. as the others?"

"It does, for sure. But..."

"What?"

"I just got fired."

"You want a drink?" someone said from behind Rigger.

He looked over his shoulder at the sound of Autumn's voice. She stood behind the couch, holding out her glass, but she wasn't offering it to him. He turned to see Pug with a silly grin on his face, nodding like a happy puppy.

"Who said that?" Rigger was startled by Katrina's loud voice in his ear. "Is that redheaded airplane woman there?"

Rigger groaned and squeezed his eyes shut. "Yes," he said. "Autumn is here."

"Why?" Katrina asked.

"She helped me work out a problem on the Dragonfly."

"I bet she did."

"Can I pick you up or meet you somewhere? I really need to talk to you."

"We're talking now."

"I want to see you," Rigger said.

"I've had a hard day, and it's getting worse by the minute."

"I'll let you beat me up."

Katrina's short laugh made him smile.

Autumn squeezed in-between Rigger and Pugsley on the couch and handed her drink to Pugsley. Rigger stood and walked toward the kitchen with the phone.

"Was she really working on the Dragonfly?" Katrina asked.

"Yes. She figured out a way to use a smaller battery."

"Good for her."

"Say it like you mean it."

"I wish she had a battery up her—"

"Nose?" Rigger said.

"Yeah, and I'm talking about a car battery."

"Why don't you and I go have a drink and talk things over?"

"Won't alcohol screw up your brain even more?"

Rigger didn't answer.

"I'm sorry, Rig. That was a low blow."

"Actually, it helps to get drunk occasionally. Some of those dead synapses come back to life and dance the matanga."

"Ha. It's the Macarena, and I'd like to see that."

"I'd like to show it to you."

"You know where the Windsor apartment building is, on forty-seventh?"

"No, but my car does."

"Apartment Seven-C, and bring some adult beverage with you."

"I can handle that."

"Try to hurry."

Rigger told her he was on his way and clicked off his phone. He slipped a bottle of Jack Daniels and four cold wine coolers into a brown paper bag. When he got to the living room on his way to the front door, he found Autumn and Pugsley talking about the new autopilot upgrade for the Tesla automobile.

"Clicker, can you guys lock the door when you

leave?"

Autumn waved goodbye but kept her eyes on Pugsley.

"Clicker?" Pug asked.

"Yeah." She took a sip. "It's a long story."

He smiled. "We've got all night."

Chapter Seventeen

Saint Tropez, France

July 4th

With the Maures Mountains as a backdrop, the hotel Le Bailli de Suffren, near St. Tropez on the French Riviera, offers a million dollar view of the Mediterranean for a modest rate of only five hundred and fifty euros a day.

Rio Lujan booked adjoining suites, with rooms on the second and third floors. The connected terraces on the third floor would provide a sweet private dining experience, with soft evening breezes off the sea for accompaniment.

He and Sasha had shared photos of each other so there wouldn't be any surprises when they met.

At La Mole, the St. Tropez International airport, he spotted her long red hair from across the terminal lobby.

Rio *was* surprised.

"Sasha!"

Other than when he'd seen her in the desert from

five hundred meters' altitude, he'd seen only headshots of her on his phone; now, he saw the whole package.

Tall and athletic, she wore a blue travel dress, with a bow on her left hip. She could have worn a peasant outfit and still stood out in the sea of common people.

Sasha adjusted the purse strap over her shoulder and waved to him.

Rio wanted to run to her but forced himself to a slow walk through the swirling crowd of travelers, while she stood her ground, making him come to her.

"It was hard to find you." He reached to shake her hand. "You're so plain, you blend in with the herd."

She laughed. "And you are, as we say, a bit of pipsqueak."

Hard-bodied, with a two-day beard and pale blue eyes, he was two inches taller than Sasha.

"I know, right? I may have to start working out...next week." He wanted to hang onto her hand, but she pulled away.

Searching through her purse, she found her luggage tickets.

"Ah, baggage." He took the tickets. "Let's go find 'em."

After he settled her in her rooms and tipped the porter, he turned to leave her so she could freshen up after the long flight.

"I'll see you on the terrace," he said.

"Okay. I just want a hot shower, followed by a stiff drink."

"How stiff?"

"Sex on The Beach?" she asked.

"Um...maybe your Russian-English dictionary needs a little calibration."

"It is cocktail, gutter-mind. Make with schnapps,

cranberry juice, orange juice, and a handful of vodka.”

“Oh, I knew that.”

She smiled. “Twenty minutes?”

“Just enough time to Google ‘Sex on The Beach.’”

Surprisingly, when Rio called room service and was connected to the bartender, the man knew exactly how to make the cocktail.

When Sasha came onto the terrace wearing a Versace gold trimmed black robe and her wet hair turbaned in a matching towel, she found Rio sitting at the table, with two tall frosty drinks.

He stood, pulling out a cushioned chair. “I ordered a double for you.”

“Wonderful.” She sipped as he took the chair across from her.

“How’s the leg?” He grimaced after tasting his drink. “Wow. I thought I had sex on the beach before, but this is dynamite.” He took another sip.

“Getting better. Did I ever thank you for saving my life in the desert?”

“I don’t think so.”

“Happy firecracker day,” she said.

“What?”

“July 4th, America’s Independence Day, yes?”

“Yes, it,” Rio said. “Thank you. When is your?”

“Russia Day, June 12th.”

“Sorry I missed it.”

She smiled. “Tomorrow, I have to find a physical therapy.”

“Therapist. I have pretty skilled hands.”

“No doubt. But I need professional.”

“All right.” He took his phone from a hip pocket. “Searching for physical therapists in St. Tropez.” He sipped his drink. “Here we go. Three professionals available. Max,

Jacques, and Dominique."

"I think I need a Dominique."

"Calling Dominique." He pointed his glass toward the beach as he waited for an answer.

Sasha looked that way to see two people parasailing behind a yellow powerboat.

"Hello, Dominique. My lady friend needs therapy." He listened for a moment. "She had an arm and a leg injury three weeks ago. Yes, she broke her right femur and right humerus." Dominique asked another question. "The casts came off..." Rio held the phone to his chest. "Five days ago?" he asked Sasha. She nodded. "Five days ago." He listened. "Tomorrow at ten a.m." He raised an eyebrow at Sasha. She smiled. "That'll be fine. See you then."

"Thank you," Sasha said.

"It's what I do."

"So, when are we going parachute flying?"

"You, my friend, will watch me parasail as you lie comfortably on your beach towel and work on your tan."

"Ha, not very likely."

"You're just dying to break some more bones, aren't you?"

"Maybe you are frightened of a little altitude, but for me, the higher, the better."

"Yes, I've seen you fly." He rotated his glass on the table. "Are they going to take the price of that Sukhoi SU-57 fighter out of your paycheck?"

"Probably, but when I find that idiot missile commander, he will find one of his missiles shoved up his fat ass."

"I think they were aiming at me."

"Then they had should better go back to school and study the differences between SU-57 and F-35. They are quite different silhouettes."

"I agree. What will you be flying when you go back on duty?"

"Not fighter jets. My commander assign me to test fly some top secret experimental aircraft."

"Have you seen it yet?"

"No. He only tell me it is not jet and not propeller. So what is there beside that two?"

"Helicopter?"

"Oh, my God. I hope not. That is way too slow for me."

"Yes." He watched her finish off her drink. "I can't see you hovering along in a chopper. Dinner?"

"Yes, I am starving." She tried to stand but collapsed back into the chair.

He reached to help her up. "I guess dancing is out."

"Two more stiff ones, and we will see who can dance."

* * * * *

At the therapy clinic, Rio sat in the waiting room, watching YouTube videos of car crashes and flying motorcycles on his phone. After an hour, Dominique opened the door to the therapy room.

"Mr. Rio, please to come in."

Inside the room, he found the smiling Sasha lying on a table under a very small white towel.

"How are you feeling?" Rio asked.

"Great." Sasha adjusted her pillow.

"I will want you for giving Miss Sasha more additional massage tonight." Dominique brushed up the towel, uncovering a well-toned, well-tanned thigh.

"Um..." Rio cleared his throat. "She...ah...I mean, we a-aren't..." He glanced at Sasha. "...that well-acquainted.”

“Oh.” Dominique was obviously embarrassed. She pulled down the towel. “I thought—”

Sasha laughed. “Just think I am crash dummy, Rio. We might to get acquainted later.”

“I did not mean to—” Dominique began.

“Not to worry.” Sasha pulled up the towel. “You show this little boy how to massage my aching muscles, and he keep eyes closed tight.”

“Well, if you think it will be all right,” Dominique said.

Rio closed his eyes and felt his way around the table to Sasha’s right side.

Dominique took his hands and placed them on Sasha’s thigh. “With your fingers, just feel this, what we call the adductor magnus of the quadriceps.”

“Uh-huh,” Rio said.

“Now…” Dominique took his right hand and placed it on her other thigh. “You find that same muscle here?”

Rio swallowed and nodded.

“You feel it soft, while this right one is a bit stiff?”

“Um…yeah, I do feel some stiffness.”

Sasha struggled to contain her laughter.

“Okay, we want this left one to made soft when relaxed, but when flexed to be stiff.”

“I see.”

“So, for one hour, more or less, in evening, you should work your fingers along here and back down for the length of the adductor magnus. Are you understand this pretty clearly?”

“Perfectly, but…” Rio took away his hands and shoved them into his pockets. “But now I just need to go run on the beach for an hour…or maybe two.”

* * * * *

On their third day at St. Tropez, after Sasha's daily session with Dominique, she checked out of her suite and moved her gear into Rio's rooms.

The next afternoon, Sasha whooped as they parasailed side-by-side five hundred feet over the crystal blue Riviera waters.

Their days were filled with snorkeling, sailing, and long walks on the beach. One bright Sunday, they rented a car and drove into the countryside, where they found a quiet inn to spend the night.

Ten days after they met at the airport, they were having lunch at a beachside café when Sasha's phone chimed.

Rio watched a smile light up her beautiful face as she read a text message. "Good news?"

"My experimental aircraft has arrived in Vladivostok."

"Oh." He toyed with his spaghetti, twirling the pasta on his fork.

"Do not do that."

"What?"

"That sad hangdog thing. We knew this to be coming anyway."

He dropped his fork. "Yeah, but so soon?"

"We had ten days." She reached for his hand. "And ten nights."

"We were supposed to have two weeks."

"If your commander text you to come fly a new type of aircraft, would you say, 'No, thank you, sir. My girlfriend is quite more important to me than flying?'"

"Absolutely."

"Then you are stronger man than I am."

"You still need more physical therapy."

She smiled and sniffed. "Maybe I not so strong."

"How about this." He handed her a napkin. "Tokyo, next weekend. And we'll talk about your new aircraft."

"Oh, you stinking Yankee spy dog." She wiped tears from her cheeks. "I knew you were only after my secrets."

"True. But I'll tell you all about our new stealth fighter."

"You mean the F-37 Talon?"

His eyes went wide.

Sasha gave him a mischievous grin and reached for his hand. "Maybe I will tell *you* about that nifty new American jet." She twisted a curly red tendril around her finger, then slipped it over her ear.

He smiled. "I guess we'll find out in Tokyo."

She stood, pulling him out of his chair.

He held her close, kissing her red lips.

"Next weekend," she whispered, "but tonight, we still have St. Tropez."

"Let's make it a night to remember."

End Book One

If you enjoyed reading Dragonfly vs Monarch: Book
One, please leave a brief
review by clicking on
the link below

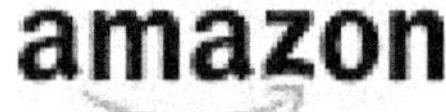

Thank you.

charleybrindley@yahoo.com

www.charleybrindley.com

Like me on Facebook → Facebook/charleybrindley

Published by Andalusia Publishing
andalusiapublishing.com

Charley Brindley is a retired coder living in the Ozarks
of southwest Missouri. He draws on his experiences in
the U. S. Air Force and extensive world travels to write

adventure novels.

Other books by Charley Brindley

Audiobook – Unabridged – Read by Liz Krane
9 hours and 4 minutes

Also available in eBook and paperback format

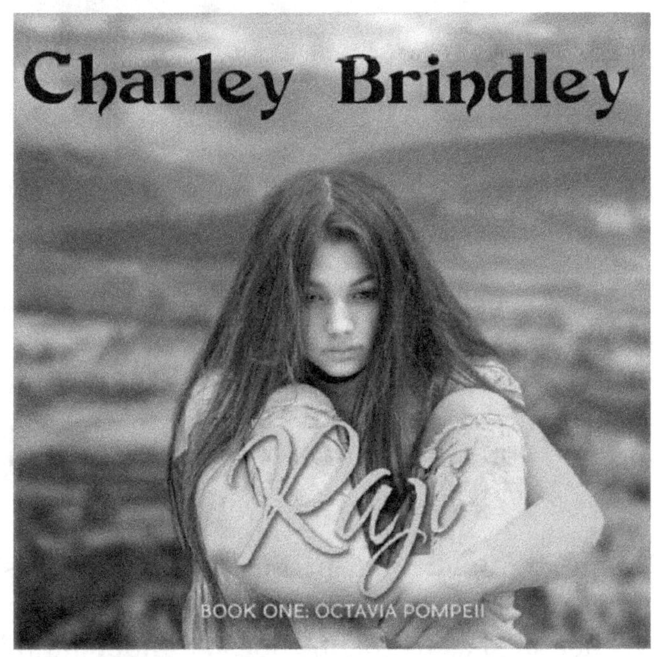

1.

Raji Book One: Octavia Pompeii

1.

Raji Book One: Octavia Pompeii

December, 1925. Vincent Fusilier finds Raji sleeping in his parents' barn. He thinks she's a vagrant and tells her she has to go. She doesn't understand English and doesn't know where she is. Over the next few months, these two teens struggle to understand each other's language and culture.

2.

Raji Book Two: The Academy

August 1926. Raji is accepted into the prestigious Octavia Pompeii Academy. She and Elizabeth Keesler are the only girls in the student body of one hundred cadets. They must endure the derision and taunts from ninety-eight boys who would like nothing better than to see the girls drop out of school. In addition to the contempt of the male students and the high academic standards set by the instructors, they must also conform to the strict disciplinary code enforced by the indomitable Elvira Gulch, Director of Development.

3.

Raji Book Three: Dire Kawa

October 1932. At the beginning of the Great Depression, schools and universities all over America were cutting back, and even closing their campuses. Raji and Fuse, like so many other young people, were to be cut adrift. Having concentrated on nothing but academics for the past four years, they weren't prepared for the brutal economic realities of a world sinking into misery and hopelessness.

4.

Raji Book Four: The House of the West Wind

Fuse returns to Burma in 1941 to look for Kayin. He left Raji behind in Virginia to recuperate from her ordeal, but she promised to join him later in Mandalay. It's been eight years since Fuse and Raji left Burma on the ill-fated training mission to Ethiopia. Since then, he hasn't heard anything from Kayin. She's probably married by now, or at least in a relationship with someone, but he has to find out, just to be sure she's all right. What he discovers at the old hotel is something completely unexpected.

5. 

Oxana's Pit

Oxana uses forced labor to operate an illegal amber mine in the Amazon. Her open-pit excavation is on land owned by Tosh Scarborough. When he discovers Oxana's pit on a satellite photo, he goes to investigate and is captured by Oxana's thugs. One of Tosh's employees, Amber Bravant, organizes a search for him. Oxana is quick to punish and even murder her slave laborers, but what will happen if she gets her hands on Amber?

6.

Ariion XXIII

Ariion Sanders, a disabled teenage girl, is inspired by a homeless man she meets in a New York City jail. The man, Cameron Littleheart St. Lawrence, has been arrested for bank robbery, but without convincing evidence, the judge is forced to release him. The bumbling bank robbers have their loot stolen from them, and they think Cameron took it. After they kidnap Cameron, Ariion hatches a plan for his rescue; however, her scheme goes awry, and she finds herself in deep trouble.

7.

The Last Mission of the Seventh Cavalry

A unit of the Seventh Cavalry is on a mission over Afghanistan when their plane is hit by something. The soldiers bail out of the crippled plane, but when the thirteen men and women reach the ground, they aren't in Afghanistan. Not only are they four thousand miles from their original destination, but it appears they've descended two thousand years into the past, where primitive forces fight each other with swords and arrows. The platoon is thrown into a battle where they must choose sides quickly or die. They're swept along in a tide of events so powerful, their courage, ingenuity, and weapons are tested to the limits of their durability and strength.

160

8.

Cian

Cian and Saxon's meeting in the heart of the Amazon is more than an encounter of two people; it's the coming together of two different worlds. Their explorations and adventures take them deep into the rain forest, then halfway around the globe in search of a peaceful place to settle down. But instead of finding peace, their shared sense of justice finds them traveling from Europe to New York, then back to Brazil, where they must confront the evil network of the ambitious and heartless Oxana, who will stop at nothing to advance her trade in endangered animals as well as women and little girls.

9.

The Last Seat on the Hindenburg

A misdialed phone number brings Donovan to Sandia's front door. He thought he was to teach Braille to a blind person, while she thought he was a disability attorney. When Donovan learns of Sandia and her grandfather's dreadful circumstances, the Braille lesson is forgotten and he embarks on a mission to help Sandia solve the several dilemmas that threaten to overwhelm her.

10.

The Sea of Tranquility 2.0: Book One

An exasperated high school social science teacher with half her senior class failing, resorts to a drastic measure, resulting in The Sea of Tranquility 2.0. Four of her students come up with a radical project to help slow rising sea levels and provide a homeland for some of the millions of refugees set adrift by wars, failing economies, and gang violence.

11.

The Sea of Tranquility 2.0: Book Two

Monica, Harry, and Caitlion try to find a way to communicate with the Jamori nomads they left behind in the Safandel Desert. While working hard to finish their senior year of high school, they're also working on details of their plan to gain funding for the Sea of Tranquility 2.0 project.

12.

The Sea of Tranquility 2.0 Book Three: The Sand Vipers

When Sikandar's homeland is invaded, he must return to defend his people. Monica defies him, refusing to stay behind, insisting she won't lose him again. The two of them, plus the Gang of Four, set off for the remote and desolate outback of Alcina Sahar, where Sikandar is certain his people have taken refuge.

13.

The Sea of Tranquility 2.0 Book Four: The Republic Monica and Sikandar, along with the Gang of Eight, open the first pipeline to siphon seawater to the Sea of Tranquility 2.0. Will it work? Scientists are divided on the theory of a nine-foot-wide pipe reaching 156 miles across the desert that'll actually pull water from the ocean unassisted by any pumps. If it works, the new City of Tranquility will flourish, if not, the desert will reclaim what little work has been done.

14.

Dragonfly vs Monarch: Book Two
The Dragonfly and Monarch are tiny drone aircrafts designed to resemble actual insects. They can flitter around military installations and terrorist camps without being noticed while they collect video data about these installations and the people in charge. On their first mission over an isolated stretch of desert, their remote pilots, one American and one Russian, are drawn into a strange struggle to survive. In their attempt to retrieve their disabled drones, the pilots discover a shocking secret about themselves.

15.

Hannibal's Elephant Girl, Book One
Tin Tin Ban Sunia

In 218 BCE, Hannibal took his army, along with 27 elephants, over the Alps to attack the Romans. Eleven years before this historic event, on the banks of a river near Carthage, in North Africa, one of his elephants pulled a drowning girl from the turbulent waters. Thus began Liada's epic journey with the elephant known as Obolus.

16.

Hannibal's Elephant Girl, Book Two
The Voyage to Iberia

Liada and the slave girl, Tin Tin Ban Sunia, sail away from Carthage with Hannibal, on their way to Iberia. Also on board is Obolus, Hannibal's prized war elephant. Not only do they have to deal with pirates and Roman galleys, Sulobo the slave master and Sukal the javelineer are on the ship, too, just waiting for a chance to exact vengeance on the two girls.

17.

The Rod of God, Book One: The Edge of Disaster

Staff Sergeant Saxon "Pagan" McKenzie and Tech Sergeant William "Choir Boy" Kabilis are involved in a nuclear accident during the Cuban Missile Crisis. Not only does it threaten to set off World War III, but it sends McKenzie and Kabilis on a journey into the first days of the Vietnam War.

18.

The Rod of God, Book Two: Sea of Sorrows

A man returns to Thailand after a fifty-year absence. When he was in Bangkok on leave from the Vietnam War, he met a girl and fell in love. After returning to the battlefield, he was critically wounded and shipped to a hospital in San Diego. After recovering from his injuries, he goes back to Bangkok, looking for Chayan, but she's not there. A year later, he returns, and one of the other girls tells him Chayan died during a typhoid epidemic. Devastated, he returns to the States, goes to medical school, and eventually starts a family. Now, after fifty years, he goes again to Bangkok, but instead of Chayan, he finds his past had been evolving without him.

19.

Do Not Resuscitate

A dying man tells his great granddaughter he has signed a Do Not Resuscitate document, giving instructions for medical personal to let him die if he's determined to be brain dead. He's invited on a long journey that he thinks is taking place in his subconscious mind as his body is being kept alive against his wishes. What unfolds before him may be an elaborate hallucination caused by the psychedelic effect of the anticholinergic drugs being pumped through his body, or are these strange and cathartic events actually happening?

20.

The queen of England is 93 years old. The process of installing a new monarch is already being organized.

Her son, Prince Charles, is the heir apparent. However, someone is attempting to alter the line of succession.

There are over 140 people in line to become

monarch. If Prince Charles is for any reason, unable to ascend, then the next in line, Prince William, will become King. If he is unavailable, Prince George will be next in line, and so on, down the list.

Evil plans are being executed.

Lady Pion Ciana Victoria Lancaster, known to her friends as 'Ciana', is number thirty-seven. William George Tindall Mountbatten is number thirty-eight on the list of Royals.

Wearing a disguise and going by the name of 'Scipio' William Mountbatten accidentally meets Ciana in a London pub.

Long ago, a general famously said, 'All battle plans fall apart upon first contact with the enemy.' That is exactly what happened when Ciana and Scipio come together.

21.

Qubit's Incubator

Catalina Saylor is allowed to work in Qubit's
Incubator on probation for thirty days. If she proves
her idea within that time, she will be allowed to stay
and try to obtain a patent on her device.

Qubit's Incubator is a work place for bright people
with good ideas who have no resources to develop
their ideas.

If they are accepted, they will be provided with a
workspace, equipment, and other benefits for thirty
days. If they are not successful within that time, they
will leave with nothing.

22. *Dragonfly vs Monarch, Book Three*

Theodore Breckinridge (Pug) and Rio Lujan join forces to rescue Autumn and **Sasha**.

23. *Hannibal's Elephant Girl: Book Three*

Liada and her friend, Tin Tin Ban Sunia, struggle to fit into their new environment in Iberia.

24. *Still Waters Run Deep*

A precious five-year-old girl is accidentally imbedded with five gigabytes of medical information.

25. *Ms Machiavelli*

The teenaged daughter of the famous Italian, Nioccolo Machiavelli, makes her mark during the Renaissance.

26. *The Last Mission of the Seventh Cavalry, Book Two*

The soldiers of the Seventh must mount a rescue mission for the stranded astronauts after they came down from the International Space Station in the escape pod.

27. *Ariion XXIX*

In the year 2219 Ariion XXIX is her third rotation as quadrant perimeter analog. She has jurisdiction along the outer beacons of our solar sphere, encompassing all ten planets and their moons, both natural and artificial. She is the 29th Ariion in a long line Ariions stretching back to the first Ariion, born in Valdacia in the year 221 BCE.

28. *The Journey to Valdacia*

A satellite cartographer has discovered on his latest photos, the ruins of an ancient city in the Sahara Desert. It has been uncovered by a recent sandstorm and Donny slips away from his job at xxx to go explore the ruins before anyone else, especially his colleague, Kelli, spots the location of what appears to be a very large city. Before he can reach the ruins, he's entangled in secret and deadly activity.